The Player

Paul Coccia

James Lorimer & Company Ltd., Publishers
Toronto

James Lorimer & Company Ltd., Publishers acknowledges funding support from the Ontario Arts Council (OAC), an agency of the Government of Ontario. We acknowledge the support of the Canada Council for the Arts, which last year invested $153 million to bring the arts to Canadians throughout the country. This project has been made possible in part by the Government of Canada and with the support of Ontario Creates.

Cover design: Tyler Cleroux
Cover image: Shutterstock

9781459415782
eBook also available 9781459415775

Cataloguing data for the hardcover edition is available from Library and Archives Canada.

Library and Archives Canada Cataloguing in Publication (Paperback)

Title: The player / Paul Coccia.
Names: Coccia, Paul, author.
Series: SideStreets.
Description: Series statement: SideStreets
Identifiers: Canadiana (print) 20200354434 | Canadiana (ebook) 20200354477 |
ISBN 9781459415768 (softcover) | ISBN 9781459415775 (EPUB)
Classification: LCC PS8605.O243 P53 2020 | DDC jC813/.6—dc23

Published by:
James Lorimer &
Company Ltd., Publishers
117 Peter Street, Suite 304
Toronto, ON, Canada
M5V 0M3
www.lorimer.ca

Distributed in Canada by:
Formac Lorimer Books
5502 Atlantic Street
Halifax, NS, Canada
B3H 1G4

Distributed in the US by:
Lerner Publisher Services
241 1st Ave. N.
Minneapolis, MN, USA
55401
www.lernerbooks.com

Printed and bound in Canada.
Manufactured by Friesens in Altona, MB in January 2021.
Job #271897

To Jo-Anne, who can now add a book by her brother to her hockey collection. You never thought that would happen, did you?

Chapter 1

Face Off

"We made the playoffs. How do we party?" Peshan whispered. He was our hockey team's left wingman. We were leaving the change room to grab our bus back to the hotel. All of the team was headed out to the parking lot.

The ride to the hotel was only ten minutes. That was nothing next to the more than two hours it took to get to Port Carling from Toronto.

I boarded the bus and got pushed along to the back by the stream of hockey players.

"You're coming. Right, Coop?" Peshan asked. Everyone got a short nickname. I was Coop, even though I liked Cooper better. Peshan, we all called Pesh. He liked Pesh better.

"I'm behind in Math," I said. "I've got to catch up." Pesh and I were sharing a room at the hotel. Really, some time alone sounded better to me than a party.

"You can spare one night," Pesh said. "You can't suck at math that much."

"I can try to get us some beer or something," another player said. I was still new to this team and found it hard to tell the guys apart. It was even harder when they weren't wearing their jerseys with their numbers. At least then I had a shot. "Coach Chug is a heavy sleeper. He'll never find out."

Really, I just didn't want to hang out with the team. They were nice enough guys. But I barely knew them. And they barely knew me. I was only the new goalie. I was the six-foot-five beefy guy filling up the crease. I had transferred onto the Great Blues mid-season because we didn't have enough players to keep my old team going. Not after my boyfriend moved away. These new guys and I might be a team now. We weren't buds yet.

The guy offering to score us beers threw his bag onto an empty seat. He dropped his phone on top. The screen flickered on. A topless woman appeared.

I looked away and could feel myself blush. Even though I didn't know his name, I now knew that the guy liked busty blondes.

"Coop's gone red," the guy laughed.

"Dude, get that off your phone," another player warned. "It's bad luck to jerk off during a winning streak. It throws off your game." He grabbed the phone. "Imagine if the Puck Bunnies looked like her!"

The Puck Bunnies were the girls that hung around us hockey guys. Normally, when talk like this started, I left. It was just the usual locker-room talk, but I didn't want any part of it. I also didn't want to see if talk turned into anything else. I'd heard a lot of weird stories about guys and locker-room pranks.

The first guy wiggled his phone in front of my face.

I pushed it away.

"Relax," he said.

I couldn't relax. Not when these guys didn't know I was gay. My old team knew. They were cool with it. I didn't know how these guys would be. How could I? There hadn't been time for me to get to know them. So I hadn't said anything about it. It wasn't that I was in the closet. I just didn't need to tell them all about me. I wanted to play hockey. Being gay had nothing to do with the game. But every time I thought about it, I started to get a headache. I tried not to think about it.

I said, "I'm good. You guys have fun."

Pesh shrugged as we got off the bus at the hotel on the edge of Port Carling. "Sure," he said. "I think I saw a store that sells beer a few blocks away. Let's try our luck there."

I nearly ran up the stairs to my room and into the shower. It felt great to take a real shower. I'd only rinsed off after the game. The showers in the arenas were another place I tried to avoid. There was something about being naked with a bunch of straight hockey players. What if they thought I was looking at them?

Not that I was too worried. I was taller and wider than any of the other guys. I rubbed my belly dry with the towel. Under the extra padding, I had muscle. If one of the guys started up, I could deck them without trying.

I pulled on my sweats. I flopped face down on the bed and opened my math book. I didn't understand this chapter. Not that I was stupid or anything. I just never got how the teacher explained stuff.

I was struggling through the practice questions when my phone pinged. The screen said my boyfriend — no, my ex-boyfriend — had a new post.

I should have been doing my homework. I shouldn't have been checking out my ex online. Still, I swiped open my screen. He looked good. Extra good. It was a topless selfie. Only his hockey pants on, and the laces on them were loose. I could see the line of hair below his belly button. He was a little sweaty.

I looked at other pics in his feed. We broke up because his family moved cities. We both knew we wouldn't be able to see each other. Not in real life. And we didn't lie and say we would try to make it work. We had one last night together. It was nice but sad. We were each other's first. I missed him.

I stopped on a photo of us. It showed us in the change room. He had his arm over my shoulders.

I heard the hotel room door opening. I shut off my phone.

"We brought the party to you!" Pesh called.

The rest of the team followed him into our room.

Chapter 2

He Scores

"I'll mix drinks," Pesh said. He took two six-packs from the guys. He dumped ice into plastic cups and poured. A cup was shoved into my hand.

I felt like all the other guys were watching me. Waiting to see if I'd join in with them or not. I took a tiny sip. I didn't like it. I decided to pretend to drink it for the rest of the night.

"Hand me a T-shirt," I said.

One of the guys grabbed my chest from behind.

"Don't be shy. The Bunnies have bigger tits than you do."

All the guys started laughing. Then they started drinking. Some of the guys were already acting like idiots. One guy grabbed my used towel and snapped it at other guys. He aimed for their butts.

"Stop acting like a homo," said a guy who nearly got hit in the sack.

"That's the most action you've seen all season!" the guy with the towel shot back.

There wasn't enough beer shared between us to get anyone even a little buzzed. But I knew they'd all say they were drunk in the morning. It was cooler that way.

"You were killer, Coop. Not a shot could get by you." Pesh clapped me on the shoulder.

"It's easy when you're built like a wall," one of the other guys said.

I was built to be a goalie. Tall. Wide. Stocky. I blocked most of the net without trying.

Some of the guys horsed around. They hit each other or play fought. I sat on the bed and was quiet. I tried to figure out who was talking. And who was who. I would have left, but I had nowhere I could go. It was my room.

Soon, pairs of guys started to leave.

"We'll get rid of the cans," one of the last four guys said. "We'll dump them in the trash outside the hotel."

"Take the cups too," Pesh said. He emptied the trash can into a plastic bag and handed it over. "We'll be kicked out of the playoffs if we're caught."

Pesh locked our door after they left. He threw himself backward onto my bed and pulled me down beside him. I never did get a T-shirt to wear. I put my arms across my middle to cover up my belly.

"That was one of the best games of my life," Pesh said. "You really were awesome, Coop."

"Thanks," I said. My size left no room on

the bed between Pesh and me. "You scored almost all the goals."

"Too bad it was an away game. The Bunnies would have gone wild. Imagine all the bouncing." Pesh cupped his hands in front of his chest and made a jiggling motion.

"I guess." I knew the girls even less than I knew the guys on my new team.

"Some of the girls like you."

"I don't think so." I felt my cheeks go warm. It was strange thinking about a girl liking me. I wouldn't even know where to start. Or what to do. Not that I was interested.

"Do you want me to introduce you? You can get pretty far with some of them. If you're not picky."

Would picking no one be thought of as being picky?

"I'm sort of with one," he said. "We're keeping things casual. No strings. She's cool like that."

Pesh's long, lean body stretched out beside mine. His cheeks, nose and brows shone in the lamp's light. I looked away. I didn't want Pesh to catch me checking him out.

"Tiana is hot. Don't you think?" Pesh asked.

"Which one is she?"

"The one with the boobs."

They all had boobs. That didn't help me at all.

"The big boobs," Pesh said. "She's curvy."

I snuck a glance at Pesh again. I peeked at the area of skin showing above his jeans. He opened his eyes.

I glanced away fast. I thought he saw me looking. I moved to put more room between us. I didn't know what to do or how to suggest Pesh go lie on his own bed. I felt like I needed to get out and couldn't think of a way to.

"You're not into girls. It's cool," he whispered.

I gulped. I think I began to nod.

Pesh rolled onto his side. He bit his

bottom lip. Slowly he reached out. He placed his hand on my chest.

I stared down at his hand on me. I'd only ever been with one guy. My boyfriend. And we'd been dating. Pesh was my teammate. He was with a girl. We weren't dating. We didn't even know each other well. And still, here he was with his hand on my chest, only inches away. I could feel my heart beating behind my ears.

When I didn't answer, Pesh started to pull his hand away.

I grabbed it and held it. He leaned in closer. He held his breath.

I knew this was dangerous. I knew there were lots of reasons not to. And I knew we were alone and he was giving me the go-ahead. And we both wanted me to take it. He dug his fingers into my chest hair. I knew we shouldn't.

Screw it. I pushed against him and kissed him. He jumped back and pulled his hand away.

I began to blurt I was sorry. I never got it

out because Pesh kissed me. A bit too hard. A bit too clumsy. Our teeth bumped. Our noses smashed into one another. But it didn't stop us.

After we were done, he went back to his bed. And we fell asleep.

Chapter 3

Delay

I woke up thirsty in the morning. And I had to use the washroom. Irony.

Pesh's bed was empty. The shower was running.

I rolled over and pushed my face into the pillow. I really had to go.

If I had known Pesh better, I might have gone in and used the toilet. I wouldn't have felt so shy.

I thought about last night. It had to be a mistake. We talked about girls. And boobs.

I'd never talked about boobs before. I'm not sure I even really talked about them last night. Pesh figured out I was gay. We kissed. Then more. We were both ready and willing. That was it. At best, Pesh was curious. He wanted to know what being with a guy was like. And there I was. It was easy. It felt good. It was just some fooling around.

Then why was I so worried about seeing him? Why did I wish he had already gone down to breakfast?

The bathroom door was open a little. A long slice of light cut across our beds.

But what if Pesh had liked last night? I knew we both liked it, you know, *that* way. But what if, maybe, there was something else?

I couldn't let my mind go there. I'd only be setting myself up to be hurt. It could only ever be a mistake.

I really needed to use the washroom. It was starting to hurt to hold it in. I groaned as I got out of bed. I pushed open the bathroom door. The toilet seat was already up.

"Couldn't wait," I called over the sound of the water.

The shower shut off. Pesh pulled back the curtain.

He said, "Throw me a towel."

I finished and grabbed the nearest towel. I handed it to Pesh.

"Sorry," I said. I didn't look at him. I guess he noticed.

He stepped out of the shower. "It's no big deal. We've changed in front of each other before."

We did a lot more than change in front of each other last night.

I turned my back to him. I didn't want him to see the reaction I was having from being so close to his wet body. I wasn't happy with my own body's betrayal. Or my lack of control over it. This morning or last night.

I went back to my bed. I was still thirsty.

"All yours," Pesh said a few minutes later. He threw the towel behind him as he walked out of the bathroom. Naked again, he lifted his bag onto his bed. He began to go through it before he got dressed in front of me.

I snuck glances. Pesh wasn't shy in the locker room. He wasn't shy out of it either. It didn't matter that we had never shared a room before. It didn't matter that we had messed around only hours before. He moved around as confident as always. He was letting it all hang out there. I wished I could have been that confident. But my body didn't look like his.

"Now that we made the playoffs, things need to change. This team is better than anyone thought. I want to be captain," Pesh said. "And I want to be made centre. That means we have to practise hard. I want to win."

My body hadn't calmed down. I stayed in bed. I lifted one knee and propped myself up on the pillows. I had to be blushing.

"We have a good chance," I said.

"A great chance. We could take this. This is one step closer to me going pro."

I sat up in bed. "Is that what you want?"

"Isn't that what every Canadian kid who grew up on skates wants? I'm not just going to want it. I'm going to do it," Pesh said. "I can't rely on luck. I'm going to work hard. I'm going to make sure the other guys do too. We're going to take it. I can't let anything stop me."

I stretched. I noticed Pesh look me up and down as I did. Now I was definitely blushing. He gave a small smirk before he finished getting dressed.

"Get cleaned up, Coop," he said. "We need our star goalie to fuel up down at breakfast. What do you think there will be? I hope it's not dry toast and muffins. We need actual food."

I still had a semi but I stood up. "We're only taking a bus ride back to Toronto."

"Get a move on. I don't want the other guys swiping all the good grub." Pesh was acting like nothing had happened.

I was fine with that. I let out a breath. Things seemed okay between us. Nothing was strange. Last night was likely a one-time thing. Something we would never talk about. Something we'd both act like never happened. Pesh got it out of his system. And I'd gotten some action. That was it.

But when I was showering, I thought about the night before. I thought about kissing Pesh.

Pesh and I might be able to act like nothing had happened. One part of my body hadn't gotten the memo.

Chapter 4

Puck Bunny

"That practice was our best so far," Pesh said. "We're going to be in amazing shape for our game this weekend."

He and I were the last two players out of the locker room. Pesh had been more friendly since the away game more than two weeks ago. At first, I thought he was sticking around the locker room because maybe he wanted to mess around again. I thought about my height and big thighs and gut. It wasn't likely. I was only flattering myself. There were a lot fitter guys to check out if Pesh wanted to. He didn't need to wait around to catch a peek of me. He could hook up with anyone he wanted. I wasn't special. He was just being nice. Friendly. Like teammates do.

"The team is coming along," I said. I lifted my bag of gear onto my shoulder. We walked up into the arena.

"Good game," a girl called. She walked down the bleachers on top of the benches.

She tossed her hair out of her face. She wore glasses with pointy frames and a T-shirt with a cat's face. Its eyes were made to look like stars in the night sky.

"Cool shirt," I said.

The girl smiled. She swept her bangs behind her ear. "Thanks. Not having much of a chest worked for me this time. The cat eyes don't end up looking trashy." She giggled. Her nose wrinkled, pushing her freckles closer together.

Pesh grinned. "Bobbi has style. For a Bunny."

Bobbi grinned back. "Call me that again and I'll kick your butt. I'm only a Bunny because you skate apes don't have any other names for us girls."

Pesh leaned in and kissed her on the cheek.

"Now that your team has a good goalie, you have a shot at winning the cup," Bobbi said.

"Sorry, you two haven't met. This is Bobbi. We're . . ." Pesh stopped.

"Figuring things out," Bobbi finished.

"I'm Cooper."

"I know. I make it my business to know the talent. I want to represent a bunch of sports stars one day. I'm getting in as they're coming up."

"What do you mean?" I asked.

The three of us began walking out of the arena.

"PR. Public relations. It's what I'm going to do when we're older. It's not enough to be a good player anymore. We've had the Wayne Gretzkys.

Those once-in-a-generation players. Now people want celebrity along with their athletes. I'm going to make stars. Or at least help make them."

"Bobbi is smart," Pesh said, "and driven."

"Like you aren't, Pesh?" she asked. "It's not enough for players to just play well. They need fame. They have to sell tickets and fill seats. To sell food. And trading cards. And action figures. And bobble heads. They need a fandom. That's where I come in. Do you follow Pesh online, Cooper? I run his social media."

I shook my head. The truth was that, since the night in the hotel, I had stalked Pesh's social media. He looked great in all his posts. I didn't realize Bobbi was doing that.

"What are your handles?" Bobbi asked. "I could give you some advice. For free, of course. I've been studying how players like P. K. Subban manage their feeds. I can help you too."

"P. K. is cool," I said.

"And famous. People know him even if

they don't know hockey," Bobbi said.

Before I could answer, Pesh bumped into a guy holding a broom. Without even looking back or saying sorry, Pesh left the arena. I guessed he didn't notice.

"You good, Dax?" Bobbi asked the guy Pesh had run into.

Dax was short but broad across his shoulders and chest. Pesh would have had to hit him hard to move a solid little guy like him.

Dax stopped sweeping. "All good." His voice was deep. It seemed to echo around us and fill up the space. It didn't boom or rumble. There was something smooth to it. Low and strong. I liked it. I wanted to hear him talk some more.

"Dax, this is Cooper," Bobbi said. "He's the team's new goalie."

I held out my hand. We shook. His grip was firm. My hand was bigger than his.

"I know," he said. "I've seen you around, Cooper. You changed the Great Blues' odds.

And you didn't start with them until the middle of the season."

Pesh pulled open the arena door. He stood inside, tapping his foot as he stared at us. Dax and I let go of each other's hands.

"I know. They weren't so great before," Bobbi said. "Cooper, Dax works in the arena. Mostly the snack shack. He makes the best hot chocolate. I don't know what he does. He makes it taste better than when anyone else does it."

"I'll need to try yours out sometime," I said.

Dax smiled. "I'll make it extra good for you. Promise."

If his hot chocolate was as deep and rich as his voice, I'd be buying a lot of it.

"I'll hold you to that," I said.

Pesh pushed the door and pointed outside. "Come on. I don't want to wait all day."

Chapter 5

One Man Advantage

"We're going to walk the main strip," one of the defencemen said. We'd just finished our game in a town called Otterville. "You coming?"

A group of six guys was heading out of the change room. Otterville had everything on a strip of only a couple of blocks.

I had hardly begun taking off my uniform. "I'll catch up later if I can." That wasn't true. I planned to head back to my room. Pesh and I were roommates again. He had requested that we room together. Part of me hoped he would join the guys. Things had remained friendly between Pesh and me. I wanted it to stay that way. I hadn't really been alone or in private with him since that night. And we had never spoken about it.

"We want to check out what the local girls are like," the defenceman added.

I gave them a thumbs-up as they left.

With the locker room empty, I took off all my gear. I stood and stretched. I had to bend my arms so I wouldn't hit the ceiling. I hung my clean clothes on one of the many hooks on the wall, and grabbed my towel, soap and shampoo.

I went to the showers. When the rest of the team was around, I'd rinse down quickly. Then I'd take a better shower at home or in the hotel. Most times, the showers in locker rooms were open concept. Sometimes there were waist-high barriers. Rarely there were single stalls.

This shower was open except for a small single stall with a bench and grab bars. It was too small for me. I wouldn't be able to lift my arms and wash under them. I didn't envy anyone who really needed that type of shower trying to use it.

I took the nozzle in the middle of a wall and turned it on full blast. I hoped these showers got hot. Most locker-room showers only got not-cold. Sure, the rink was chilly, but under all that padding and equipment, I sweat a lot on the ice. I didn't feel the cold the same way the fans would. It sunk in after. A hot shower after a game was a treat.

The steam started to build up from the water. My lucky day! Another win. An empty change room. Hot water. I lathered up my hair. I began humming as I washed.

I jumped. Another shower head had turned on. I rinsed the shampoo out of my hair to look.

When I wiped the water from my face,

I saw Pesh. He turned on the shower next to the first one. He moved down the line, turning all the nozzles until he stood in front of me. The steam got thicker.

"Need help washing your back?" he asked. We stood only feet from one another.

I shook my head. "What are you doing?"

"You know," he said.

"Here? Someone could walk in. Someone could see us."

"That's what the steam's for."

As much as the other night had been fun, this was different. We could get caught. This could end really badly. And then there were other reasons.

"You're with Bobbi," I said.

"We're keeping things casual. It was her idea. No strings. No rules. I'm free. So is she."

When I didn't answer, Pesh said, "You worry too much. Didn't you like last time?"

I nodded. "Yes."

"Unless something is bugging you, then,

why stop at once?" Pesh bit his bottom lip. "Is something bugging you? Did I do something wrong?"

"No. It's . . . just . . . I don't know."

Pesh smirked. "Do you want to kiss me again or not?"

I'd thought about kissing Pesh a lot. I wanted to. But . . .

"We'll kiss a little bit here. The risk will make it hot," he said. "Then we'll head back to the motel. It will be good. You'll see."

Chapter 6

He Shoots

After Pesh and I finished in the motel room, I got up from the bed to take another shower. A real one. Pesh came into the washroom when I was under the water stream. I heard him brush his teeth.

I peeked around the curtain, looking for a towel.

"Don't be so shy," Pesh said. He looked at my reflection in the mirror. "You don't need to cover up so much. I like how you look."

I *was* shy about how I looked. He was right about that. I had love handles and a gut. I wasn't sure why he liked my hairy body or big thighs or any of it. But he did.

There was a different problem though. "The bathroom is kind of small. I'm already crouching to use the shower. It might be easier if we took turns in here."

Pesh rinsed. Spit. Headed for the door. He didn't say anything.

"Only because of the space. Not anything else," I said.

"Calm down," he called back. "Don't turn things into a drama."

"I wasn't —" I began, but didn't want to scream. I dried off and went back into our room with the towel around my waist. The lights were off. I could see Pesh in bed with his back to me. I pulled a pair of underwear on under my towel and got into my own bed.

I worried he was upset. I didn't want him thinking I didn't like being around him.

Especially the next time we fooled around. If there was a next time. I worried I'd messed things up. All because the bathroom was too small and I was too big.

"Coop?" I heard through the dark. "Would it be weird if I got into bed with you?"

I exhaled. So he didn't think I was being a drama queen. I began to nod and realized he couldn't see me. I snapped the sheets back.

I heard him get out of his bed. He slipped in beside me and pulled the covers over us.

He cuddled against me. "You can ditch your underwear. If you want."

I wriggled and pushed them off. When they were down my calves, Pesh used his foot to shove them off me and onto the floor. He moved his head onto my shoulder. His leg slid between mine.

"This okay?" he asked.

As an answer, I put my arms around him and held him. His head tucked under my chin. In not too long, he was asleep. His hair smelled good. His body was warm. Not too hot so we got sweaty. But nice, like blankets on a cold night. I kissed the top of Pesh's head.

I shifted. Pesh made a little noise. He moved in closer to me and squeezed me a tiny bit. I turned onto my back. One of my arms stayed under his head. His body fit along my side just right.

With my ex, any time we kissed or did anything else, it was always in a rush. We didn't want our parents walking in. Our parents were cool with us dating. But it didn't mean we wanted them to catch us in the act.

With Pesh, like this, I didn't worry about anyone walking in. The deadbolt was on. We were safe. At least, safe in the motel room. It's not like we were letting the team or Bobbi or anyone else know we were fooling around.

I grabbed my phone. At first, I squinted from the screen being too bright. I swiped to my camera and made sure the sound was off. I held it out and took some photos. With each one, I was afraid the flash would wake Pesh. He didn't even squint.

I looked through the pics. I snapped some more. There were a few I really liked. I decided to take one more. I kissed his forehead and snapped. Pesh mumbled and lifted his face toward me. I kissed him on the lips, both our eyes closed. I snapped another. That one was my favourite.

I scrolled through the photos. It was stupid of me to take them to begin with. But there were a few good ones. I kind of liked them all. Pesh and I looked like we were together. A couple. I smiled. I knew I should delete the photos. I selected them and went to hit the trash button.

Pesh made a happy little noise again. He rolled over and pressed his back against me. He pulled my arm under him and held my hand. His fingers slid between mine.

I rolled into him. I put my other arm over

him. He nuzzled in. Big spoon and little spoon. Just like a couple.

I made a little happy noise too, before I fell asleep. My phone was on the nightstand. I hadn't deleted a single photo.

Chapter 7

Winning Streak

We couldn't lose. We played a semifinal series of seven games that month, travelling between Toronto and Otterville. We won, taking four in a row. We were on to the next level. The final round!

Pesh and I were on to the next level during that month too. After the last away game, we began fooling around any time we could. It happened mostly before or after practices. As I got more used to the idea of someone catching us, I liked the risk. There was something kind of wrong about sneaking around. There was something kind of thrilling. Anyone could walk in. It made it all a little more epic. I was still nervous, but I didn't stop to think about it as much anymore. And we never really talked about it either.

Of course, Pesh and I tried to be smart about things. We tried to pick spots where we'd hear if anyone came in. We never took off all our clothes unless it was in the showers or our hotel room. There was other stuff too. Instead of ignoring each other, we acted like friends around the other guys. Pesh pointed out it was more normal if everyone thought we were buddies. I thought we were, anyway. And, maybe slowly, I was becoming part of the team. I wasn't just the new guy or the new goalie anymore. I was Coop who had helped get the Great Blues to the finals.

"Pesh. Coop." Our defenceman nodded at each of us. He was the last guy besides us in the change room. He reached out. We took turns fist-bumping with him before he left.

The day's practice had gone well. Pesh was pushing us all hard, even though he wasn't captain. I ended up drenched in sweat under my uniform. I'd need to do a load of laundry and leave my gear to air out.

Almost as soon as our defenceman left, we heard the door open again.

He stuck his head back in. "Pesh. Your girl is out here."

"Thanks, Brian," Pesh said.

I'd have to try harder to remember Brian's name. In my head, he was defence twenty-three.

"She's like, college hot," Brian said. "You know? Like, smart-chick hot. I bet she gets freaky. Smart chicks know stuff the rest of the Bunnies haven't even thought of."

I gritted my teeth.

Pesh laughed. "She *is* smart, so she's *extra* hot."

"Guess you're not a rack man." Brian cupped his hands in front of him.

Pesh smirked. "Can't have it all. See you tomorrow at practice."

Brian left again. Pesh and I shoved more stuff into our bags. Mine wouldn't zip shut.

"You don't like that kind of talk, do you?" Pesh asked.

"What talk?"

"Guy talk. Locker-room talk. You made a face."

I didn't think I had made any kind of face. Maybe I had. "There's a lot more than how someone looks that goes into making them hot," I said. "The Bunnies are real people with real feelings. They're not just chests and butts."

"Are you just talking about the girls?" Pesh winked at me. He moved like he was going to grab my ass. "You've got more ass than any of the girls. Don't worry."

I smacked his hands away. "Gross."

"You know you're hot too," Pesh teased. "I asked Coach Chug if we could room together for the rest of the season. I was tired of asking every away game. He said yes."

"How did you manage that?" I asked. Most of the time, guys rotated room partners unless there was a good reason not to. I tried again to push my stuff into my bag, but it wouldn't zip shut. I gave up.

"We played an undefeated round. We made the finals. I told him it was good luck. He believes in that stuff as much as any of us."

"Getting lucky isn't the same as good luck." I turned to face Pesh. With a glance around to be sure, I kissed him. A quick one. "We could fool around. If we're fast. Do you want to?"

"Oh, I want to." Pesh bit his lip. "But Bobbi is waiting."

"Oh."

I didn't mind hiding things with Pesh. At least, not a lot. I did mind lying to Bobbi. I didn't know her that well. But she and Pesh were a thing. Even if not a serious one. It still wasn't right if he was her boyfriend. When I thought about Bobbi, I felt my stomach twist. It hadn't stopped me though.

"Bobbi knows she's not the only one. I'm not the only guy she's been seeing either. We agreed we didn't want to know what the other one did. No details."

"Does that cover you and another guy?" I asked.

"What's the difference? It would be the same whether it was you or some girl."

"Am I just *some* guy?"

"No. Is that what you think?"

I shrugged. I didn't know what I thought. Pesh and I hooked up. I knew that. It was always clear that's how it was. I had never even asked if he was bi or what. I didn't know if I was even the first guy he'd been with. I thought I was. But sometimes he was so cocky.

I didn't pretend we were together. I knew

we weren't. And, really, it wasn't like when we got together we went all the way. It was a little sex. And it was good sex. But it wasn't more. Not even if we cuddled in bed after. Not even if I held Pesh all night. I couldn't pretend we were together. My head and stomach started to hurt.

Pesh said, "The only person I'm doing this stuff with is you. Not even Bobbi and I do more than kiss."

"I didn't know that." My head and stomach calmed down.

"Now you do."

"But —" I began.

"Are you unhappy?"

"No." It was true. I was having more fun with Pesh than I had since my ex. When I saw Pesh, my heart raced. Plus, there was good stuff about not dating him. We didn't need to do big talks about how we felt. We didn't need to deal with being the only gay couple people knew. When we hung out, it was chill. If Pesh texted and I was tired, I said so. He wouldn't worry I was angry at him for something that happened earlier. If we were feeling like fooling around, we said that too. Then we'd hook up. It was electric. It was exciting. It was easy. And it left me happier.

"We good?" Pesh asked. "Bobbi's waiting."

I nodded.

Pesh's eyes dropped. My jock was sticking out of my bag.

I went to shove it in deeper.

"You should wear that next time we're alone," Pesh said. "You look great in it."

I felt warm. "Right. The way my belly sticks out in front of it is sexy."

Pesh's cheeks went a little red. I'd never seen him blush before. "I like it. Wear it for me? At least once?"

"It will stink after practice. It gets all sweaty and gross," I said.

Pesh's cheeks went more red. "I sort of like how you smell after a game. It's manly." He wouldn't look at me.

"Oh," I said. I never thought someone might like that. "I could do that. If you really want."

Pesh looked me in the eyes. "I do," he said. "And we really need to go. Bobbi."

I took a second to adjust myself before I followed him out.

Chapter 8
Hat Trick

Bobbi was tapping away on her phone as we came up the ramp from the change room.

"Good job, boys," she said. "The way you're playing is working. We have a bunch of new followers, Pesh. The video I posted of today's practice has more likes than normal. I tagged you in it too, Cooper."

"Thanks," I mumbled.

Pesh leaned over Bobbi's phone. "Who are the new followers? Scouts?"

"A mix. A few girls. You have some fans, Cooper. Female fans," Bobbi said. "They left some comments. They think you're tall and cute."

"How can they tell he's cute with all his gear on?" Pesh asked. "Tall, maybe."

"He is cute," Bobbi said. "Girls know. You don't need to get red, Cooper. It's a fact."

"Right." I patted my belly. "I don't really think so. But thanks."

"You'd be easier to cuddle up to than this bag of bones." Bobbi pointed at Pesh. "He's all elbows. You can't get comfortable near him. Cooper, you really do go red! See? Cute!"

Pesh punched me softly in the shoulder. "Should I be getting jealous?" he asked Bobbi.

Bobbi gave me a wink. "Should you? I could trade up. Goalies are better than forwards any day. Way more loyal." Bobbi giggled. "But Cooper isn't interested. We better stop before he goes any redder. He'll burn right through his clothes."

"I'd love to see that," Pesh laughed. He winked at me when Bobbi wasn't looking.

I shifted from foot to foot. I didn't think I could look at either Bobbi or Pesh. I knew it was just joking around. But I didn't know what to say.

"Sorry." Bobbi stopped laughing. "I was serious about you being cute. I didn't mean to embarrass you."

"It's nothing," I answered.

"Let me make it up. We'll take you home," Bobbi offered. "I drove."

"That's okay. It's easy to take the streetcar." I wasn't sure I could last an entire car ride alone with Bobbi and Pesh. I couldn't pretend to be fine all that time. Although Pesh and Bobbi had decided they would see other people, I was the other person. I couldn't accept a ride from her. It would have been too strange. Standing there with them was already bad enough.

"Another time," I said.

Bobbi opened her mouth.

Pesh cut her off. "Let it go."

"Another time," Bobbi agreed.

Bobbi took Pesh's hand. They began to walk out of the arena.

"I'm going to grab an energy drink. Don't wait," I said when we reached the vending machines. I put down my bag and began to fish around in my pockets for my wallet.

"Later." Bobbi waved over her shoulder.

Pesh held up his hand and waved once.

With Bobbi and Pesh gone, I sat on the bench nearby. I didn't want a drink. I wasn't even thirsty. I wanted to give Bobbi and Pesh enough time to get good and gone so I wouldn't bump into them again.

I looked up. "Hey," I called across the arena. "Hey! Hot chocolate!"

Dax stopped. He was carrying a ladder. He leaned it against a wall.

I left my bag by the bench and jogged over to him. "How's it going, Dax?"

Dax grinned. He spoke in his deep, rich voice. "For a second I thought you thought my name was hot chocolate."

"I remembered your name."

"So I see." He kept grinning.

"What are you doing?" I asked.

"I was going to change some light bulbs. A few are flickering. Would you even need a ladder to reach?"

"I'm not that tall," I said.

"You're pretty tall. It's a good thing."

"It's not bad. So when do you work the snack bar? I never see it open. I still need to try that famous hot chocolate of yours."

The metal window grille was pulled down on the snack shack.

"We only open when there's an event. Like a game," he said.

"I play on game days. No time. How do I score one?"

"You could ask Bobbi to get you one."

I shook my head. "She's too busy watching

Pesh and posting online. Plus it would get cold by the time I changed."

"I guess you have to be nice to the guy behind the counter. He might hook you up."

I asked, "How do I go about that?"

"Knowing his name was a good start."

I reached for the ladder. "How about I help him carry this? Where does he want it?"

Dax pointed. "Over by the vending machines. Near your bag. But you don't need to do that."

"Hey. I've got to be nice to the guy in the snack shack. He's the real power around here."

"That's right. So does that make you the muscle?"

I set up the ladder. "I don't enforce. I block shots. I protect the net. I'll hold while you climb."

Dax took the steps with care. He changed two bulbs. When he climbed back down, he stopped partway. We were eye level.

"Did I get in good with the snack shack guy yet?" I asked.

"Almost," Dax said before he climbed all the way down. "There are still more bulbs to change. Are you going to stick around?"

"Sure. Where do you want this next?" I asked, grabbing the ladder.

Chapter 9

Barn Burner

"Bring it in, boys!" Coach Chug called across the ice at the end of the next practice. "Skate harder! Hustle!"

We crowded around our team's bench. Coach Chug stood on the other side of the door.

"You've been playing well. The new changes," he looked at me, "are working. I don't want to see you slacking off in practice just because last round was easy."

"I won't let that happen," Pesh said.

Coach Chug nodded. "I know. Which is why I have two bits of news. The first. Peshan has been acting like a leader since we made finals. As we're between captains, he's earned the title. He'll play centre from here on in."

The guys cheered. A couple slapped Pesh on the shoulders. I gave him a thumbs-up from where I stood.

"The second piece of news. We should not have gotten this far into the playoffs. Not from how we performed the first half of the season. It wasn't until Cooper joined us that things turned around. Good job, son," he said to me. Then he spoke to the rest of the guys. "You've all proven yourselves to be a strong team with strong players. You've worked hard. Now that we're in the finals, it's being noticed. Scouts have contacted me. There's interest. You need to play even harder to get into a higher league. I'll be sad to see some of you go."

Pesh looked over at me. He returned the

thumbs-up. Even though Coach mentioned me, this was Pesh's news. He was the star. He scored the goals. He worked harder than anyone else. He was captain and, now, centre. A scout would draft him. He'd be playing at a higher level next year. On a different team. In a different league. Things between him and me would come to an end. But only if we all kept playing the way we were. And Pesh would make sure of that. He still needed a decent team to make him shine.

"Hit the showers. You stink," Coach finished. "We'll get in one more practice this week before our first game of the final round."

The team bumped against one another as we headed off the ice. Pesh moved in beside me.

"Scouts! If we get drafted, we could end up playing pro someday," he whispered. He was almost bouncing on his skates.

"Stop bouncing. You'll slip and fall," I warned. "You have a good shot at being drafted."

"You too."

I shook my head. "I don't think so. You're the one getting breakaways and assists."

"You block almost everything that comes at you," Pesh said.

"I don't even know if I want to play in a higher league. I just like to play. I never thought about moving up. It's never been my dream." Besides, goalies just stood in the crease. We didn't get noticed unless we were bad. We were rarely stars.

"Well start thinking about it," Pesh said. "We need to do anything it takes to make this happen. Anything."

Despite the good feeling in the change room, we all changed quickly and left. Everyone seemed to want to get home for the night.

"My place," Pesh said as we finished up.

"I have to go home. I'm still behind in Math," I replied.

Pesh smirked. "You'll be behind no matter what. My place."

I knew what that smirk meant. It meant we'd celebrate. Just us. In private.

"My mom and dad are out for dinner." Pesh headed toward the arena doors.

As we went across the parking lot, Pesh pressed a button on the keys in his hand. A white SUV's lights flashed and the horn beeped.

"My parents let me borrow the car. Hop in." Pesh popped the trunk and dumped his bag. He headed to the driver's side.

I put my bag beside his and slid into the seat beside Pesh. The car was nice. Leather seats. Clean. Even the mats. It looked like no one had ever driven it.

"Can you believe it?" Pesh said as he drove. He barely stopped at the first stop sign. Or the second.

I grasped the grip on the door.

"A chance at being drafted. I'm getting this. I'm going pro." Pesh drummed the steering wheel as he swerved around cars. "This wouldn't be happening if it wasn't for you. Our team sucked with our old goalie. We might as well have pulled him at the start of every game."

"You're giving me too much credit," I said. I clutched the grip tighter. I used my other hand to grip the seat.

Pesh swung around a parked car. "I'm going to give you a lot of credit when we get to my place. You deserve it. Things between us, they seem right. Don't you think so?" He put a hand on my thigh and squeezed.

"Keep your hands on the wheel, Pesh. Ten and two. Focus on the road like you'd focus on a game."

"I am!" Pesh gripped the wheel with both hands again. He changed lanes. A car honked at us. "Why do you think I'm getting through traffic so fast?"

We stopped at a red light. I knew I shouldn't encourage Pesh or his poor driving. Still, I said, "I thought it was because you were eager to give me that credit."

Pesh grinned. He stepped on the gas as soon as the light turned green. We shot forward.

"Oh, I'm going to give you so much credit," Pesh said. "You won't know what to do with it when I'm done with you."

Soon, we pulled into the driveway of a house. A big house. Pesh's home made my house look tiny. The bushes and shrubs out front had been covered for the winter. Pesh popped off his seat belt. He almost yanked me toward him.

"We should go inside," I said against his lips between kisses. "You don't want the neighbours to see."

Pesh's head shot up. He looked around. No one was in sight. I hadn't meant to scare him. "You're right." Pesh threw open his door. He yanked the keys out of the ignition and ran up the walkway.

I followed him inside.

"Crap," he said. "My parents are here.

They weren't supposed to be."

I looked around. The walls were white but the floors and furniture were dark wood. It was polished and super shiny. The wood had a red tone to it. Even though it was dark, it felt warm and rich. There were two big carved chairs with lots of detail. Flowers, leaves, birds and other animals. They were like thrones. Their backs curved and the arms curled. They looked like they'd be comfortable. Their cushions and the curtains on the front windows were really fancy looking. The patterns had a lot of details. Gold threads ran through them. And the place was clean. Nothing was even dusty.

"Peshan? Are you home?" A short, round man came to greet us. I figured he was Pesh's dad, Mr. Cooray. "You brought a friend. Welcome. Your mother and I are having tea. You'll join us."

"This is Coop," Pesh said. "You and Mom were supposed to be out."

"Called off last minute," Mr. Cooray said. "Nice to meet you, Coop."

"Your house is really nice," I replied.

Mr. Cooray pointed around. "We had everything shipped. From back home. It belonged to our families. Our lines go way back. We even have white ancestors."

"Dad! You can't go around telling people that. It's wrong." Pesh turned to me. "I'm sorry. They're from Sri Lanka. Some people care about stuff like that." He shot a dirty look at his dad.

"British Sri Lanka," Mr. Cooray added.

"That's bad too, Dad," Pesh said. "You need to stop."

"What's wrong with being proud of where and who we came from?" Mr. Cooray asked. "We're from a wealthy line. Our family ranks very high. One day all these family riches will be yours, Peshan. You should know their value."

A woman only a little taller than Mr. Cooray came up behind him. "He knows, dear," she said. "Leave it be."

I held out my hand. "Mrs. Cooray. I'm Cooper. I'm the goalie on the Great Blues."

Mr. Cooray rolled his eyes. "Hockey. Do you want to be a star too? Like my son?"

"Coop doesn't want that," Pesh replied.

"Smart," Mr. Cooray said. "As much as we may want them, we don't always get our dreams."

This time Pesh rolled his eyes. "I'll have you know that Coop and I have scouts watching us. We're making it to the pros."

"You need to study," his father told him. "Not waste all your time on some game. There's no future there. You need to be smart."

"I am smart. This is business. If I go pro, then I'll get other deals. I'll invest my money. We'll be rich again. Like you were in Sri Lanka. Richer, even. And, better, I'll be famous."

Mr. Cooray looked like he was going to say more. His wife patted his shoulder. "Leave it be," she repeated softly. "Will you join us for tea, Cooper? It's a special blend. Imported."

I heard Pesh huff.

"I need to get home. I have homework," I replied.

Mr. Cooray stood taller. "You're not only tall and fair-skinned. You're *very smart*. Thank you for being friends with my son."

"Dad!" Pesh glared at his father before he turned to me. "I'll drive you home."

"It's okay. I'll call a ride." I pulled out my phone and hit a few buttons. "Done. I'll just grab my bag. It was good to meet you." I held out my hand to each of Pesh's parents.

They gave me smiles as we shook.

"I'll walk you out," Pesh offered.

"It's really okay."

I stepped out onto the porch. Pesh followed and closed the door.

"I'm sorry. This was embarrassing. My parents are . . . they're my parents. They're stuck in an old way of thinking."

"They're nice."

"They're a lot."

I smiled. "So are you sometimes."

"We were going to, you know."

I nodded. I knew.

"I'm going to make it up to you," Pesh said. "*I* owe *you* now."

I grinned. "I don't want to miss my car."

Pesh popped the trunk. I got my hockey bag. I waved at him before he went inside.

My phone vibrated. I pulled it out to make sure my ride was still coming.

It was a text from Pesh. My ears and cheeks burned from reading it. He'd sent details of what he thought he owed me.

I stood at the end of the driveway. I held my hockey bag in front of me as I thought about what we were going to do the next time we got the chance.

Chapter 10

Home Ice

I didn't catch the door in time when I got home. It slammed shut behind me.

"Kitchen!" Mom called.

"I've got dinner ready!" Dad yelled.

I dropped my bag as I walked down the hall.

No matter how much we cleaned our house, there was always animal hair. There were always a lot of crates and cages. Both my parents were vets. They often brought sick animals home. They cared about people's pets almost as much as the owners did. Sometimes, during the night, I'd take turns giving an animal medicine or taking them outside. If it was okay, I let one of the cats or dogs sleep on my bed. We didn't have a pet right now. I knew it was only a matter of time before one of their clients surrendered an animal they couldn't care for and we'd keep it.

We weren't shiny-wood-and-spotless-house people. We weren't fancy-fabric people. We were a-couch-that-someone's-cat-had-scratched people. We were animal-food and water-dishes and pill-bottles-all-over people. Our house would never be fancy. Or have imported stuff. We could never have white walls. It wasn't how we lived.

Dad cleared a spot on the table for me. It was a slow night. We only had two cats and a dog visiting. They were curled up in their crates.

"Before you ask, it's chili. Not pet food," Dad laughed. He made that joke every time he made chili. It always made me smile.

"I made garlic toast after you texted you were coming home," Mom said. "Too bad your plans changed."

I got my fair skin from my dad's side. I got my height from my mom's.

I ate. Mom and Dad filled me in on the animals. Their evening meds would probably keep the cats and dog sleepy. They wouldn't require much looking after.

"So big news at practice," Dad said when he and Mom finished discussing treatment options for the visitors.

"For Pesh it's big. He wants to go pro."

"But for you?" my mom asked.

I had never really thought much about it. I played hockey because I loved it. And I was good. Was I pro hockey good? I didn't know. Even if I was, did I want it? There weren't any out pro hockey players. Did I want to go into the closet to make it into the pros? I didn't love the idea.

"I know you were closer with your old team," Dad said.

"Your boyfriend was with you there too," Mom added. "That had to make it easier. Does anyone know you're gay on your new team?"

"They don't need to know," I said.

Mom went to the freezer. She pulled out a bag of frozen balls of cookie dough. Dad set the oven.

The door to the dog's kennel was open. I leaned over and patted him. He rolled a little to show me his tummy. "I don't know them well enough," I said. "I don't want to be the team's gay mascot. Or worse. Hockey guys aren't known for being gay-friendly. The way they talk about girls, I can only imagine what they'd say about me."

"Your whole life, it's going to be your call whether to tell people or not," Mom said. "But it might make a difference if you let your team know."

Dad nodded. "No matter what you decide

to do, it will be the right choice. And we'll be right here."

I looked down at my empty bowl. "Pesh knows. I didn't need to tell him."

"Isn't that good?" Mom slid the tray into the oven.

It wasn't bad. It just was. I bit the inside of my cheek as I thought about Pesh and me. I knew I could have told my parents about us. Everything about us. Even about Bobbi. They wouldn't have told me to stop. They wouldn't make me feel bad or tell me I was wrong. They'd ask if we were being safe and using protection. They'd listen mostly. That was them.

The leg of the chair I was sitting on had chew marks. A clump of pet hair had drifted into the corner. The kitchen was small and smelled like baking cookies.

"You're good enough to be drafted," Dad said. "You're better than good enough to be a member of your team. They're lucky you joined."

I felt my shoulders relax. I didn't know they had been tensed up. I was glad Pesh's parents had been at his place. It was nice to be in my own home. As much fun as sneaking around and fooling around was, I was glad not to have to be looking around to see if anyone was watching.

My phone buzzed. I pulled it out to see if it was Pesh. It's not like I was waiting for him to say anything more about his parents. It's not like I thought it would be anything but some flirty message.

I looked at the screen. The chili went solid in my gut.

"What's wrong?" Mom asked.

Bobbi had texted me. She wanted to come over.

There was no other reason she'd text me. She had to know.

Chapter 11

Dangle

The door to our house was barely open before Bobbi came in.

"I'm Bobbi." She gave a small wave to my mom and dad. "I hope you don't mind me stealing Cooper for a bit."

"Not at all," Mom said. "Did you want to come in? I'm going to check on our guests."

"Guests?"

Bobbi took off after my mom toward the kitchen. Dad raised his eyebrows at me.

I shrugged. I didn't know what to expect. I tried to tell Bobbi I was busy and tonight wasn't good. She insisted. I told her I had a headache and my stomach hurt. It was true. *No* was not an answer she'd take. After ten minutes of text arguing, I sent her our address. If she was going to yell at me about hooking up with her boyfriend, at least it would be done with.

But Bobbi only seemed curious. A little bit pushy. But not angry.

"Oh!" I heard her exclaim.

She was on her knees on the kitchen floor.

Mom opened one of the cages. A white cat with yellow-green eyes woke up. The cat lifted her head. It began rubbing her cheeks on Bobbi's fingers. Then it purred.

"She likes you," Mom said. "That does it. When animals like you, we like you."

Bobbi laughed. "That's all it takes? I'm sure this kitty likes everyone."

"She's been asleep all night."

The cat stood and arched her back.

She climbed onto Bobbi's lap.

"I told you," Mom said to Dad and me. "We like her."

"My dad has allergies. We can't have pets." Bobbi fixed the blankets in the crate and the cat stepped back inside. "Ready to hit the road?" Bobbi asked me. She jingled her keys.

Even though Bobbi didn't seem mad, I was worried about hanging out alone. How much did she know? How much did she suspect? I didn't want to go but I didn't know how to get out of it.

I nodded and put my coat on.

Bobbi's car looked used. It was neat, but not clean like Pesh's. There were a bunch of papers across the back seat. An empty bubble tea cup was in the holder.

Bobbi stopped at all the stop signs. She leaned forward in her seat to check all directions.

"Where do you want to go?" she asked.

"I don't really go out this late."

"There's a coffee and dessert bar by the airport. Their pie is the best. It's not the best tasting in town. But it's a big slice. And the servers let you sit as long as you want. Sound good?"

"Sounds fine." Any other time, it would have been great to be going out on a school night. I liked pie. The place sounded cool. But Bobbi wasn't my friend. We didn't know one another that well. Then there was Pesh. He was all we had in common. That's what worried me.

Bobbi stopped at a red light. "There's something I want to talk about. Something serious."

I gulped. "We don't need to go out for that. You can just tell me."

Bobbi shook her head. "No. We need pie."

We barely spoke the rest of the way.

When we went inside the diner, Bobbi asked for a table away from the other customers. There weren't many to worry about. The guy at the cash told us to grab two plastic-covered menus and sit where we wanted. Bobbi chose a booth at the back. She shifted the table to give me more room to slide in.

A server came over with water in two plastic glasses. They had a lot of cracks running up them.

"A large cream soda, right, sugar?" he drawled at Bobbi. "You want one too?" he asked me.

"No. Thanks," I replied.

"Let me guess," the server said to Bobbi. "You're going to have the chocolate silk pie. Extra whip."

Bobbi nodded. "Thanks."

"What are you going to have?" he asked me. "We have pies and cakes. There's some bars left but they're dried out by now."

"Then I'll have pie."

"We got banana cream, Boston cream, coconut cream, peanut butter and mile-high lemon pie. Someone just ordered the last slice of chocolate silk." He paused. "I'm kidding. I'd find you a slice of that any day." He winked at me. "Tall and easy to make blush. Where did you find him?"

"The hockey rink," Bobbi said.

"Last place I would have looked. So what's it going to be?"

I could feel my face burning.

Bobbi said, "Bring him the same. Extra —"

"Whip." The server patted my shoulder as he walked away. He returned quickly with a tumbler of cream soda for Bobbi.

Bobbi took a big sip before she said, "Let's get down to it. We need to talk about what's going on with you and Pesh."

Chapter 12

Grinder

"Nothing's going on with us," I choked out.

Bobbi unwrapped her straw and plunked it in her glass. "I already know. Pesh told me everything. I spoke to him after you left his place."

The server returned and slid two plates in front of us. The slices of pie were almost too big to fit on them. The whipped cream looked like a mountain. He filled up Bobbi's water glass from a pitcher he carried.

"Can you leave it?" Bobbi asked.

"I'm not supposed to."

"But will you?"

"I'm not supposed to." He put the pitcher down on the table and patted my shoulder again as he walked away. "But sometimes I forget."

"It's not what you think," I blurted.

"I think you're not taking this seriously enough," she said.

"It's not serious. It's only some fun. We're only fooling around." I felt myself get sweaty. I was sure stains were forming under my arms.

Bobbi shook her head. "Do you really believe that? You've got a shot here. Don't you want to take it? You'd be playing one level below pros."

I blinked. Pros? She was talking about hockey?

"We haven't been made offers," I said.

"Yet. Unless you two mess up the next couple of games, you're good. Even if you lose, you'll get noticed. I'm not wrong."

"I've only ever played for fun," I said.

"You need to start playing for more. You're a great goalie. Push yourself. Who knows where you'll go?" Bobbi drank more soda. "And I'm the girl to help you. You've got the skills. I've got the brains. Let's talk about Cooper as a brand. Let's talk about your image. Your style. How do we sell you? How do we make you famous?"

I looked down at my hoodie and jeans. I didn't think I had much style or anything else.

"Some flashier clothes," said Bobbi when she saw where I was looking. "Some good pics on your profiles. Everyone is going to know you. Girls will be all over you. Guys will be all over you too. Hockey is big. And gay guys love it. Even if they don't, they'll love you. You can have a whole fan base no one else has snatched up. Your following could be huge."

"What?" I asked.

Bobbi put down her cup. "I'm usually right about these things. You're gay? Aren't you?"

I stared down at my pie. I hadn't tried it.

"I guessed," Bobbi said.

"Well, yes. I am."

Bobbi took a big bite of pie. "I thought so. Your parents know too?"

I nodded.

"I told you I'm usually right about these things. So you're the gay goalie."

"I don't know if I want to be the gay goalie. A lot of people think hockey is the most homophobic sport in the world."

Bobbi sipped. "Isn't it time that changed?"

"It doesn't mean I'm the one to do it."

She refilled her cup. "It doesn't mean you're not. Try the pie."

I took a bite. It was good pie. I took a second bite.

"There are fans out there waiting for a gay player. We'll establish a big online following. This can make you more of a draw to scouts. You'd bring something different to their teams. You'd bring fresh fans. It helps you look good.

You're tall, strong and great at the game. Gay or not, fans will relate to you. They'll like you," Bobbi said.

I shook my head. "And what about the trolls? What about people who post hateful stuff online? Guys don't come out in hockey for good reason. I don't want to be famous for being gay."

She stirred the straw in her drink a while before she said, "Fame and a following are great. But they're only numbers. And that's a way to get power to do what you want. You could change hockey. Think about what it would have meant to you if you had seen a gay hockey player growing up. Or someone bi or trans or non-binary. It says that hockey is for them too, just as they are. Don't kids deserve that? Don't they deserve to see someone like them?"

I poked at my pie. Everything she was saying sounded right. Kids did deserve all that. But was I the best person? Was I ready to risk being bullied or treated strange in locker rooms? Would it even make a difference? Could I actually change anything?

Bobbi must have read my face. "I'm not trying to force you to tell anyone you're gay. I'm not trying to get you picked on. It's only an idea. How about we go shopping? New clothes. A few photos. I can increase your following. You'll get a sense of what I do."

"We could try that."

"Great. Give me your names and passwords. I'll fix your feeds." Bobbi pulled out her phone.

I stared at her. Did I really want to trust her with my social media? She would be able to see everyone I followed or messaged. "I'm not sure."

"I'm not going to force you. If you don't trust me, that's okay."

"Is this how you're going to get me to agree?" I asked.

"No. You'll agree. Or you won't."

"So you're not going to push at all?"

Bobbi sighed. "I can't tell you what to do. Not on this. It's your life. Even if you don't want my help, this is a shot at something big. Bigger than making the pros even. A chance too good to pass up. You're a star. Don't be afraid to shine."

"Don't be afraid to shine? I thought you were tough. I thought you wouldn't take *no* for an answer," I said.

Bobbi reached across the table with her fork and stole a bite of my pie. She'd finished hers. "I am tough. It doesn't mean I'll make you do anything you don't want."

I knew I should think better of it as I said, "Give me a pen before I regret it. But I don't want you posting about me being gay unless I say so."

"That's not how I do things. I'm building you up. I'll take care to do it right. You'll see." Bobbi held out her hand.

I reached across and we shook.

"I think this means we're friends now. That

means I get the rest of your pie." She pulled my plate to her.

"That's the only condition?" I asked.

"That and we talk about guys. There you go, getting all red. It takes almost nothing. So, rugby players. Hot, right? So wide and muscled and rough and grrr."

I released a breath. "Totally. Very grrr." I reached across for some of my pie.

Chapter 13

High Stick

It was just after ten o'clock when we left the dessert bar. Bobbi insisted on paying.

"I bugged you until you came out," she said as we got into her car.

"I have money."

"It's my treat."

My phone buzzed. It was Pesh saying he hoped things earlier weren't too weird. I thought they were weirder for him than me.

Bobbi's phone lit up. She started the car

before she checked it. "Pesh is texting. I'll answer later." She shoved her phone into her purse.

I knew I shouldn't ask, but I couldn't help myself. "How are things between you two?"

"Good."

"But, like, what's going on between you? How does it work?"

Bobbi swung out of her parking spot and made a left out of the lot. "We're dating."

"So you're his girlfriend?"

"No. I don't want to be his girlfriend."

I turned my head to stare at Bobbi. She kept watching the road. I had thought she and Pesh were a couple even if casual. Boyfriend and girlfriend.

Bobbi sighed. "We talked about it. Don't get me wrong, Pesh is a good guy. He's even great sometimes."

"But?"

Bobbi shrugged. "But he's focused on hockey. He wants to be famous. He can do it too. I like that about him. I'm the same. I want my career above everything else."

I asked again, "But?"

Bobbi laughed. "It's that clear? But I don't know what being a couple would look like with him. Would I be a good girlfriend? Would he be a good boyfriend? And . . ." Bobbi stopped and bit her bottom lip, ". . . it feels like Pesh is always on. You know? He's always playing the game. He acts like he's just one of the hockey guys. He makes the same dumb jokes and says the same dumb things they all do. That's not him. He thinks he has to do that. Especially since they're all white and he's not."

I'd seen Pesh talk about the Bunnies and heard him joke with the guys. I thought it was so no one would guess about him and me. But Bobbi had noticed it too. I could hide being gay. Pesh couldn't hide being Sri Lankan. I knew some pro players were treated really badly because of how they looked, who they were. People posted stuff online. Bad stuff. They said mean things. The same people might post that kind of stuff about a gay goalie.

"It's hockey," Bobbi said. "I don't pretend I know what it's like for him. But I've felt like I don't belong in the rink too, unless I'm there to cheer on some guy. I'm a girl, but I'm not some Puck Bunny. I don't fit in with hockey either." She sighed. "I've tried to talk to him about it. He won't talk about anything serious with me unless it's building his fandom. It's hard to get close to someone like that."

We were both quiet for a few minutes.

Bobbi changed her tone. She sounded bubbly like the pink cream soda as she said, "Things are mostly good. Pesh and I hang out. We're free to do what we want. We don't owe each other anything. It's easy. We don't have to worry about the boyfriend-girlfriend stuff."

Neither did Pesh and I, for different reasons. It was only fooling around with us. Being boyfriends wasn't something we would consider. I understood what Bobbi meant about Pesh being on though. About not being able to get close to him. I understood a bit more about why, maybe. Then I thought about Pesh getting in bed with me. And pulling my arm around him. And the pictures of us. Maybe he did let his defences down a little. Maybe when he was around me. Then he wasn't hiding or putting on the show.

Bobbi said, "Pesh is fun to hang out with. There's something there between us. But I'm not sure what it is or isn't."

Even though Pesh said he and Bobbi weren't having sex, I wondered if hanging out was the same for them as it was for Pesh and me. "So, hanging out?" I asked. I hoped Bobbi would take the hint.

"A lot of TV. Mostly hockey. Sometimes a movie. Something to eat."

"And that's it?"

Bobbi laughed again. "Nosey. Oh, come on! You blush over almost nothing."

"It's my skin. I go a little red and it's the

only colour anyone sees," I said. I rubbed my cheeks — like that would help.

"Since you want to know so much. We make out. We haven't done much more. Pesh never pushes it," Bobbi told me. "I wish he'd make more of a move. I know he believes in luck. He probably thinks if we do it, it'll throw off his game. He's doing too well since you started playing with him to risk ruining his season."

"So you're okay with not going any further?"

"I'm not sure. I think I want to do more with him. I want to know what that's like. Maybe then I'd know what there is between us. I must sound so stupid and slutty."

I shook my head hard. "Not at all. You're talking to a gay guy. Isn't stupid and slutty what we're known for?"

We both laughed. I thought about how alike Bobbi and I actually were. We both wanted to know where we stood with a guy.

The same guy. We both liked being with him. And not being with him. It wasn't just messing around. It was kind of a mess. But we both liked the mess.

Bobbi swung into my driveway. "I like talking to you. We should hang out more. We'll make good friends."

I agreed. But hanging around Bobbi could be dangerous. What if she found out about me and Pesh? Still, I liked her. And having her as a friend seemed like it could work.

"I think so too," I replied.

I got out of the car and waved as Bobbi drove off. There was a note on the front door asking me to check on the animals before I went to bed.

I went to the kitchen. As soon as I turned on the light, I heard a thumping. The dog lifted his head and kept wagging his tail. The cats stayed curled up like cushions in their crates.

I undid the lock on the door of the dog crate.

I got myself a glass of water and sat down at the table. The dog put his head against my thigh. His tail swished across the floor behind him.

"Hey, boy." I scratched behind his ears. He licked my hand. "If only all guys were as easy to figure out as you."

Chapter 14
Hoser

Pesh called the team over to my net. They circled around.

"It's the start of a new week and it's the first game of the finals," he said. "There are only minutes left. We're behind by one goal. We need to tie it up. Let's push it into overtime. We can still win."

I lifted the cage on my helmet. "They're a good team. We've only scored twice."

"They've only scored three times."

"We might not win this one," I said.

Pesh glared at me. "We have to win. I have to win. I'll score the goals. You worry about keeping them from getting past you. Just us two can do it."

The rest of the team stared at each other. We weren't a team if it came down to two players. Pesh made it sound like we didn't need them. They'd played as hard as we had. The other team was tough. This wasn't like the last series. This would be a hard round.

Pesh skated away.

"Guys?" I said before the rest of the team took off. "We won't ever win working alone. I can't stop every shot. I need you. Let's see if we can tie it up. If we can't, we win the next one. Together." I held out my glove.

The other guys nodded. They put their gloves on top of mine and we cheered. Without Pesh. They took turns slapping me on the shoulder pads before they took their positions.

The last few minutes made no difference.

Pesh had a short breakaway. Their team stole the puck. No one scored. The clock ticked down. We lost. Three to two.

When we got into the locker room, Pesh threw his gloves at the benches.

"Calm down, dude," Brian said. "It's one game."

"To you!" Pesh yelled. "We need to work harder!"

I said, "We played our best."

"We still lost!" Pesh yelled. "We need to play better than that."

I turned to the rest of the guys. "It was close. We're pretty evenly matched with the other team. Next week's game, luck will be on our side."

"Luck isn't enough." Pesh pushed off his skates. "Be early for practice tomorrow." He stripped down. He left his gear in a heap on the floor. He muttered as he stomped away, "We even had home ice."

I started taking off my gear to follow him.

Brian grabbed my shoulder. "Leave him. He needs to cool off."

I got out of my uniform with the rest of the team. I passed Pesh as I headed to the showers.

"Be quick. I'll be waiting in my car," he said. He didn't stop or give me a chance to answer. He was still dripping from his shower.

A guy named Dale snuck up behind a wingman named Chris. Dale began pretending he was humping Chris from behind.

"Get lost! Don't be gay!" Chris exclaimed when he realized why everyone else was laughing.

"Don't pretend you didn't like it," Dale said.

"I'd rather be riding the bench than riding your mom!"

"More like riding my dad!" As he walked away, Dale high-fived Brian, who was a few shower heads over. Brian was the only guy not laughing.

I knew I had to get out of there. I lowered my eyes, soaped up, rinsed down, changed. That shower was all business. I threw my stuff into my bag and headed out, saying bye as I did.

Dax was mopping the floor in the arena. "Someone spilled their drink. Mopping is one of the perks of the job. Good game."

"We lost," I answered.

"Both teams played well. This will be a great final series. You'll get them next time. Don't worry."

"Thanks. Sorry. I've got to go. Pesh is waiting."

Dax rolled his eyes.

"What?" I asked.

"Nothing. I shouldn't have done that."

"No. What?"

Dax held the mop handle and leaned on it. "I'm not a fan. He's a strong player. He's captain. People seem to like him. But he's kind of a jerk."

"He is not!"

"Maybe." Dax began mopping again. "He bosses you and Bobbi around. And the rest of the team. When he wants to go, he expects you to be ready. He gets upset when he has to wait. He doesn't even see people he doesn't think are worth his time. He seems like a jerk to me. A total hoser."

"He's not that bad," I said. "I have to go."

Dax wrung out the mop. "Did he tell you to hurry up?"

I didn't answer.

"See," Dax said. "Scoot along."

"It's not like that. He's really not that bad."

"I only know what I've seen." Dax dunked the mop in his bucket. He began cleaning the floor again. "Go on. You don't want him to get mad."

I opened my mouth but just shook my head. I wanted to stay and talk to Dax. But I didn't want to argue about Pesh. I stepped over the wet spot on the floor with one stride.

Chapter 15

Save

Dax was wrong. Pesh didn't get mad. He already was mad.

"The team isn't worried. Why would they be? A scout isn't looking at any of them. It's you and me. Brian and the rest of them are making us look bad," Pesh ranted. He ran a stop sign. Luckily, there were no other cars in sight.

I kept quiet about the sign. Not like I could have gotten a word in. He'd started complaining as soon as I was in the car and hadn't stopped.

"If we lose, no scout is going to see we're good players," Pesh continued. "I'll have to wait until next season and hope to get drafted then. Another year wasted."

"I don't agree with you," I got in when Pesh took a breath.

"What? How could you not agree? They're making you look bad too."

I shook my head. "It was a hard game. Both sides played really well. It wasn't ours tonight. You're the only one acting this way. But you're not the only one who is playing hard."

"But —"

"No. All you're doing is turning the team against you. Everyone is upset. No one will play well. No one will want to be on the ice with you," I kept going. "You need to say sorry."

"But did you hear Brian?"

"Brian didn't yell at everybody. Brian isn't fighting with me right now."

Pesh stopped at the next sign. And the one after that. After a few blocks he said, "I'll think about it."

"We can't win every game, Pesh. We'll win the series. Keep your eyes on the prize. Turn right," I instructed. "My house isn't far." I wasn't looking forward to Pesh seeing my home. His was clean. It had fancy furniture and fabrics and art. Ours had sick animals and chewed-up chairs. It smelled like a vet's clinic.

Without warning, Pesh jerked the steering wheel. We screeched into a parking lot beside a park. He turned off the engine and popped off his seat belt. He was on me almost instantly.

"Wait!" I said as Pesh began lifting my shirt and undoing my jeans.

He yanked open my pants and began kissing my neck. "We should have done this before the game. We play better after we fool around."

I pushed Pesh back. "Getting laid has nothing to do with winning. You know that, right?"

"Come on." His dark eyes were warm and big and open. He slid a hand up under my shirt. "You know it helps. You can't say our game isn't better after we've played together." Pesh leaned back and took off his shirt. The light from the street lamps made him glow. I could see the muscles across his stomach. I saw my round, hairy belly.

I moved his hand away. "We're in public. I don't feel good about this. Anyone could see us."

"So?" Pesh asked. "That makes it better. I'll be quick. You're ready. You want it."

I did my pants back up and pulled down my shirt. "Not here. Not now."

Pesh dropped back into his seat. "Whatever." He found his shirt and yanked it back on.

"Don't be like that."

"Like what?" he asked.

"You know it's a bad idea. We're out in the open."

"I'm not being like anything."

"I'm going to walk home. It's not far," I said.

Pesh stared out the front window. He crossed his arms over his chest. "Whatever."

I pushed a button on the dash. The trunk opened. I got out and grabbed my hockey bag. I began to walk. It was cold, so I zipped up my coat. I left the lot and turned toward my house.

I was almost home when headlights shone from behind me. I heard a car pull over. Its door opened then slammed.

"Wait," Pesh called.

I turned.

He jogged over. He grabbed my wrist. "I don't want you mad at me."

I looked down at his hand. He wasn't wearing a coat or even a sweater.

"I like you," Pesh whispered. "I don't always show it how I should. But I do like you."

"We're teammates. I know."

Pesh slid his hand into mine and held it. He leaned up and kissed me softly on the chin. Standing on tiptoe, he kissed me again on the lips. "More than teammates."

"We're in the middle of the street," I said.

"I didn't mean for things to happen like that just now." Pesh let go of my hand. "It's cold. I'm going to go. I'll say sorry to everyone before practice. You were right."

He didn't let go of my hand. Normally he'd be looking around to make sure no one saw us.

I sighed. "We're sharing a room again in a few days. Right?" I asked.

Pesh smirked. "For sure."

"Okay," I said. I knew I probably still sounded angry. I kind of was. But I wanted to stop fighting more than I wanted to be mad.

"Okay?" Pesh asked, still smirking.

"Yeah. Okay." I smirked back.

Chapter 16

Between The Pipes

Four days after that fight, Pesh and I sat together on the bus to Grand Bend for the second game of the finals.

Once we arrived at the hotel in Grand Bend, Pesh and I got our keys and rushed to our room. The game was starting soon. There was only a little bit of time before we had to get to the arena. But with how we went at each other as soon as we were alone, we only needed a little bit of time.

Without much talk after, Pesh and I hurried to the arena. We geared up and got on the ice, still pumped from our secret pre-game action. Pesh looked back at me from the blue line and grinned. I smiled back. Then the puck dropped and we were in action again. Although a very different kind.

I ended up playing a shutout. Pesh scored the only goal of the game.

Coach Chug rounded us up and took us to a pizza place near the hotel. We took up tables in different corners of the restaurant. The staff could barely keep up bringing us food. As soon as they set down a pizza, we'd have it finished. They left pitchers of pop on the table. Those didn't last long either.

Tired and happy and full, our team went back to the hotel.

"Do you want to? A victory lap?" Pesh asked when we were alone. He gave me a big wink.

I thought about it. "I'm okay."

"Me too. Which bed do you want?"

I pointed at the one nearest the door.

"Cool." Pesh kicked off his shoes and undressed.

I headed to the bathroom to brush my teeth. The bedside lamp was on when I got back. Pesh was in my bed.

He threw back the covers. "You don't mind. Do you?"

I pulled off my clothes and got in beside him. "It's cool."

"You're tall. You might like the whole bed."

"No. This is nice." I put my arm over Pesh.

He turned out the lamp. In the dark, he kissed me and curled into my body. I held him closer. It was like the first time we'd slept in the same bed. I smiled to myself.

I was nearly asleep when Pesh said, "I want to ask you to do something for me."

Maybe Pesh hadn't had enough earlier.

"Will you wear something for me? At practice. When we get back tomorrow. I think it would be hot," he said.

My brow wrinkled. "What are you asking? Like another jock?"

"Sort of," Pesh said. He moved around. The lamp turned on.

Pesh got up and went to his knapsack. He rifled through. He tossed something at me.

A pair of red lace panties landed on the bed beside me. I picked them up with two fingers.

"They're new," Pesh said.

"They're for women." I held them up. I had never touched women's underwear. "There's barely any material."

Pesh sat down on his bed. "Do it. Please? I really want to see you in them. I want to know you were out there on the ice. All your manly hockey equipment on. A sexy secret under that. Only you and I will know about it. It will be between us."

I turned them around. "It's a thong. I can't even get these on without breaking them."

"They'll fit. You'll look great. For me?" Pesh asked.

I shook my head. I was probably as red as the panties. I couldn't even imagine squeezing into them. "I'd feel stupid. I won't even fit all my parts in them."

"I know." Pesh gave me that grin. "That's part of what will make it hot." He got into bed with me again. "I'll make it up to you. Promise. I'll do something special for you."

I already felt stupid and he'd only asked me. What if another guy on the team saw me? I'd have to be super careful. But Pesh was already so excited. I threw the panties at him.

"Fine. I'll give it a try. Turn out the lights."

He shut the lamp off and pushed me onto my back. He got on top of me.

"I thought we were done," I mumbled around his mouth as we kissed. I grabbed his hips and flipped him. I got on my hands and knees over him.

"I did too." Pesh grabbed my shoulders and pulled me against him.

"How are you going to make it up to me?"

He gripped the back of my head. "There's a condom in my bag. Do you want me to get it for you?"

I was silent. We both stopped. Neither of us moved.

"Coop?" he asked.

I asked, "Have you done this before? With anyone."

"No. But I've thought about it. A lot. I want to. With you."

"It's not as simple as having a condom. Other stuff has to happen first. I don't want to hurt you," I said.

"I'm not afraid."

But I was. He was trusting me. I stayed frozen.

Pesh slid out from under me. When he came back, he pressed a condom into my hand.

★★★

After we had finished in the bedroom, we each took a shower. Separately. Pesh went first.

When I came out of the washroom, Pesh was in his bed. I went to my bed to fix the sheets.

"What are you doing?" Pesh yawned. "Get over here."

When I got in, he lifted his head. He pulled my arm under it like a pillow. He pressed his back against my side.

"Are you okay?" I asked.

I felt Pesh nod. "Are you?" he asked.

We'd just gone all the way. This was more than just some fun. This wasn't just fooling around. This was different. I felt good but I didn't know if I was really okay. Things had changed. They'd become more.

I kissed Pesh behind his ear as softly as I could and hugged him to me. My stomach grumbled loudly.

Pesh laughed. "I'm hungry too."

"I really want a sandwich," I admitted. I

knew I could never admit the other stuff.

"Room service," Pesh suggested. "A turkey sandwich would be amazing right now."

"A club sandwich would be even better."

He rolled on top of me. I put my arms around him and stroked his back.

The kitchen was still open. Club sandwiches would arrive in a half hour.

Pesh settled down on top of me. I kissed the top of his head and kept stroking his back until there was a knock at the door with the food.

Chapter 17

Five Hole

We were on a winning streak over the next week. We'd taken the next two games. If we won one more, we were the champions.

Pesh and I repeated *that* night after our last win in Grand Bend. He must have liked it the first time. It was easier the second time together. He had a box of condoms. I bought a bottle of lube from the grocery store in town.

I wore the lace underwear. More than one time. Pesh got extra turned on when I did.

I sort of liked how they made me feel too. That was a surprise. I liked having a secret. Not that Pesh and I didn't have a really big one.

With a week off before our next game, Pesh called double practices every day. Before and after school, and all day on the weekends. He set up drills. I sat out some of the practices. I didn't need to do things like speed skate as a goalie. I had to get my homework done and study and rest. I was worried everyone was getting worn out. But Pesh didn't ease up. On the other hand, he didn't argue or put down anyone if they sat out or skipped any of the practices.

I sat in the bleachers, struggling through my math homework during Friday's after-school practice. Dad and Mom had tried to help me. I was lost again. I'd even gone for extra help. The teacher only confused me more.

Pesh was doing drills. We were the only two Great Blues players there. The arena's manager had agreed we could use the ice whenever it wasn't booked. More games, especially playoff games, meant higher attendance. That meant more snacks got sold.

"Why are you doing it that way?" Bobbi leaned over my shoulder and took my pencil. I hadn't heard her come up behind me. "It's easier like this."

I looked at what she'd written. "Way easier! Thanks!"

"Some teachers call that way cheating because you don't do all those steps. But it makes it simpler."

I worked on the next question and showed it to Bobbi.

"You got it!" she said. "I'm bored. Want to go across the street to the coffee shop?"

I closed my book. "Why not?"

Bobbi waved as we walked toward the doors. "Dax! Hey!" she yelled across the arena. "Grab your coat! We're going across the street!"

"I can't!" he called back. "Working!"

Bobbi ran across the arena. She dragged Dax back with her. "You get breaks. Don't you?" she asked. "Take one. You know I usually get my way. Let's save the middle part. Agree to come." Bobbi kept a firm grip on Dax's arm.

"Fine," Dax agreed. "But I only have a little time."

Inside the shop, we ordered and got the last table by the window. Bobbi let me treat. It only took a small argument. Dax tried to hand me some money.

"You'll give me one of those magic hot chocolates. We'll be even," I said.

"I guess I'll always be the hot-chocolate guy."

"What's wrong with that?" I asked.

Dax shrugged. "Nothing. Sure. I'll pay you back with a hot chocolate."

"It better be as good as all the hype."

"It's only a hot chocolate."

"With marshmallows?" I asked.

"Of course."

"Can I get extra?" I smiled at Dax.

"You're a goof," he laughed.

I loved his laugh even more than his voice.

I tried to think of something to say to make him laugh again.

"I should get back. I need to keep my job." Dax stood. "Thanks for the drink."

"Any time," I said.

Bobbi leaned back in her chair once Dax had left. "So. Dax?" she asked me.

"What about him?"

"What do you think about him?" she asked.

He'd been right there a minute ago. Why was she asking me now? "He's a good guy."

"That's it?"

"I like his voice. It's deep. Like an echo," I said.

"Nothing else?"

"What else is there? The hot chocolate?"

Bobbi rolled her eyes. "Boys," she muttered. "I've booked you a haircut."

"This is playoff hair." I knew I needed a cut. But playoffs were an excuse not to bother.

"Don't even start with that. And we need to go shopping. I'm all for a relaxed look. But can your pants at least fit you right?"

"My pants are fine," I said.

"You don't have an ass in them. Don't worry. The new pants won't be super tight. You know you're good-looking. Right?"

I pulled the bottom of my sweater down. "I'm not a model or anything. I'm okay at best."

"You've got the height. You've got the blond hair. Even the bit of scruff on your face is good. Let me fix it so everything is extra good. I won't change too much. Just enough to make you shine a tiny bit more."

"A tiny bit. That's it."

"It's all you need," she said. "I don't want to change who you are. I want to help everyone see it."

"And I'll look good?"

"You already look good. You'll look better. Look at your last post. Look at the numbers." Bobbi held out her phone to me. "They're boosting."

There was a photo of me in the crease

squirting water into my mouth. I had never had so many likes before. My ex had even made a comment saying he missed being on the ice with me. The post had only been up a couple of hours.

"How did you manage this?"

"I told you I'm good at what I do. Here's the plan."

Bobbi laid it out. None of it involved me making it public I was gay. None of it made me sound like a hockey player wrapped in a rainbow or a dumb jock. Bobbi wanted to show off that I was a great player first. Then we'd figure out how to bring in that I was gay.

"I've got some notes in my bag," she said. She bent over. Her shirt rose up. I saw her underwear above the waist of her jeans. She had on a red lace thong. It was the same as the one Pesh had given me.

"Your, um —" I pointed. My mouth and throat went dry.

Bobbi yanked her shirt down and

straightened up. This time, she went red.

"You don't need to look so shocked," she finally said. "They're underwear. I wouldn't even normally wear ones like these. Pesh gave them to me."

"Does he," I swallowed, "normally give you that kind of stuff?"

Bobbi swirled her strawberry lemonade around the cup. "If I tell you something, you need to promise not to tell anyone. Okay?"

I nodded. I took a drink but my throat still felt parched.

"We did it," she whispered. "He's been really happy lately. We were hanging out. I told him we should. Hey, Cooper, is everything all right? You don't look so good."

I felt the tips of my ears burn. I began to sweat. I knew I shouldn't ask. I knew I couldn't stop myself. "I'm fine. Did you, uh, find the answers you were looking for?"

"It helped a little."

"Helped?"

"It's not like it's a one-time thing. Pesh and I have been together a while now. A few more times and maybe I'll figure out more stuff. Are you sure you're okay? You're white. More than normal." Bobbi reached out to pat my hand.

I jerked it away. I didn't want her to touch me. Not now that I knew she'd touched Pesh like that. And he'd touched her. And me. I wished I hadn't finished my drink. I felt like I might throw up. "Tired. Lots of practices. I overdid it today."

"You weren't even on the ice."

"The week caught up with me. I'm going to go home and rest."

"I'll give you a ride. I'll let Pesh know. I'll swing back later to get him."

"No. Really. I'm okay. I need to get home," I said. I grabbed my backpack and tossed my cup in the garbage.

"Bye." Bobbi stayed seated.

Once I was far enough away and sure Bobbi couldn't see me, I jogged back to the arena. I needed to see Pesh. Now.

Chapter 18

Shirted

I stood at the boards and waved my arms. Pesh came over.

He pulled off his helmet. "Everything okay?"

"No."

Pesh waited for me to keep speaking. Then he sighed. "What's up?"

"Remember the underwear you gave me?"

He gave me that smirk and ran a hand through his hair. "How could I forget?"

"Remember the underwear you gave Bobbi?"

Pesh's jaw dropped. He reached for the door. "That rink rat who cleans the arena is around here. Let's get to the change room. I don't want anyone to hear." Pesh pushed past me.

Once we were inside the locker room, he braced a folding chair against the door.

"You're mad?" he asked.

I shook my head. I wasn't happy. I wasn't sure if I was angry though.

"You knew Bobbi and I are a thing," Pesh said. "That didn't stop you from getting with me."

"You said it was only me."

"It was only you."

"Why didn't you tell me?" I asked.

"I didn't tell Bobbi about you."

"You two agreed not to tell each other," I said.

"Right. So why would I tell you? What was

I supposed to say? That I'm going to sleep with my girl?"

"I don't know. Something." I pinched the bridge of my nose. I could feel a headache behind my eyes.

"Coop, I thought you understood what was going on."

"I thought I did too. I thought we were friends. I thought you liked me. You said you liked me." I let go of my nose.

"I do like you. If I didn't, we wouldn't have fooled around."

Was it really that clear to him? He liked me. I liked him. He liked Bobbi. And we could all do what we wanted. But it all meant nothing? "You gave Bobbi and me the same underwear. I shouldn't have found out this way."

"I don't get why you're upset."

"You should have told me," I said. "You should have warned me."

Pesh threw his hands up in the air.

"I didn't know I had to. Fine. I'm sleeping with Bobbi. Better?"

And he was sleeping with me. I balled my hands into fists. I was angry now. I didn't want to be near Pesh. "Not better." I yanked the chair away from the door.

"What do you think is between us? And how did you get that idea? It wasn't from me." Pesh held out his arms. He looked like he might try to hug me.

I shoved his arms away.

"What do you think I owe you?" he asked. "Tell me what I did wrong."

"I don't know," I said. I really wasn't sure now. Were we just fooling around? Was it more? The lines were all blurred. My fists were still balled up. I didn't want him to touch me. "You know what? You're right. You didn't do anything wrong. You don't owe me anything. You don't have to tell me this stuff. But I thought we were friends. Not just with benefits." I threw open the door and stormed out of the locker room.

"Coop, don't go."

I stomped down the hall.

"Where does this leave us?" he asked.

I called back, "The same place we always were. Nowhere."

I left the arena and was a few blocks away in almost no time. I shivered at the streetcar stop. I knew Pesh wouldn't pass by here. Neither would Bobbi. I wasn't upset with her. That didn't mean I was ready to see either of them. My phone was shoved deep in my backpack. I didn't want to hear it or feel it. If anyone tried to contact me, I'd check when I was good and ready.

"Hey." Dax walked up beside me.

"Hey." I pushed my hands into my pockets.

"I saw you in the arena. By the time I punched out, you were gone." He stood beside me. We stared down the tracks.

"I needed some air."

Dax nodded. "It can get pretty old in there."

I shifted from foot to foot. The night air was cold.

"Is everything okay?" Dax asked after a bit.

"Fine. Why?"

"The way you left. The way you were staring into nothing when I got here," Dax said.

I sat down on the bench and huffed. My breath puffed out in front of me into the night.

Dax sat too. With his wide shoulders and my tall and wide everything, we touched. There wasn't enough room on the bench not to.

"It's okay if you don't want to talk about it," Dax said.

"Thanks."

Dax pointed down the tracks. "Streetcar."

We got on silently. Dax and I were the only passengers. He sat beside me. Our bodies were even closer against one another in the seats. He didn't try to chat. He didn't pull out his phone. Or a book. Or stare out the windows. Or look bored. His body was like a heater. It warmed me up just sitting beside him.

Dax reached over me to press the button for his stop. I liked the way he smelled when he leaned in.

"This is me," he said softly. His voice reminded me of warm fudge brownies. "Whatever it is, Cooper, it will pass."

"Thanks." I fist-bumped Dax before he left.

Chapter 19

Blue Line

I got off the streetcar and walked to my house. I opened the front door and looked around. Everything was shiny. The floors were vacuumed and washed. The counters and tables were clear of vet supplies. I would have let Pesh come inside now. Well, before, I would have. Right now, he could stay wherever he was. My fists balled up again.

"What happened?" I asked Mom and Dad.

"A miracle," Mom said. "All the animals

are healthy. Even the office is empty tonight. We instructed the staff to do a deep clean. Your dad and I did the same here."

"But that means no money," I pointed out.

Dad laughed. "The health of our patients is more important than money. Don't worry. We always do fine. It's good to do a clean like this every so often."

"Did you eat?" Mom asked me.

I sat and slipped down on the wooden chair. They'd even polished. A lemon scent came up from the table. "I could use something."

Mom grabbed stuff from the fridge. Dad looked over her shoulder. He got a bowl.

"We've got everything for a super deluxe chopped salad," Mom said.

"And I baked oatmeal pie," Dad added.

"Is there ice cream?" I asked.

"Why even make oatmeal pie without ice cream?" Dad reached around Mom, who was taking more things out of the fridge.

He got the pie and put it down on the counter. I thought of the pie slices from the dessert bar. I thought of Bobbi. And red lace. I pushed them from my mind.

Soon I was eating a salad made with all sorts of veggies, ribbons of lunch meat and cheese, nuts, pickles and hot peppers. The whole bowl was for me. My dad slid over a wedge of pie with ice cream. The ice cream hadn't begun to melt and drip down yet.

I ate slowly. Mom and Dad traded a look with each other. After practices, I normally wolfed down my food.

"What's going on, Cooper?" Dad asked. He moved his chair closer to Mom. She leaned against him.

I didn't want to lie, so I said, "Hockey drama." I bit into one of the peppers. I liked spicy food and could feel it burn.

"Your mom is the one of us who knows hockey," Dad said.

When hockey was on, it was usually Mom

and I who watched. Dad made us popcorn, read reports and made sure the animals were resting.

"Are the practices too much? Making the finals can be a lot. You can tell Pesh to cool it," Mom suggested.

I chose my words carefully. I didn't want to tell them everything. Maybe someday in the future. Not tonight. "Pesh has been a lot lately. He does these plays, but he doesn't tell anyone else what's going on. I think I should be told what's going on instead of figuring it out on the fly."

"Even if he is the captain, a team needs all the players," Mom said. "You need to try to get the puck going in one direction by working together. You can't do that if you don't know what direction that is."

"Are you sure this is about hockey?" Dad asked. "Or is this because you're a goalie? Does he not think you should know what everyone else is doing because your job is to mind the net?"

I shook my head. "The salad is good."

"Did you try telling Pesh how you feel?" Mom asked.

I could have laughed. I had tried to tell him earlier. Or I thought I had. Right now, if he was trying to talk to me, I wasn't picking up my phone.

Mom cut herself a thin slice of pie. She gave my dad the first bite. "Maybe you two need to have it out."

☀ ☀ ☀

The next day I skipped practice. I ignored Pesh's texts and calls. If Coach called a practice, I'd show up. I didn't need to see or talk to Pesh in between. I decided I wouldn't go to Pesh's practices.

That didn't stop me from thinking about Pesh most of the morning. Pesh had been right about a few things. We weren't boyfriends. We weren't dating. I knew he was with Bobbi. I knew it was just some fun between us. Then why did it feel like he'd done something wrong to me? If he didn't need to tell me about him and Bobbi, why did it feel like he lied and hid things? We'd been lying and hiding from everyone. Why did I feel so stupid?

Mom called me. I went downstairs.

Bobbi was standing there. She was wearing mittens that looked like cat paws. They even had claws on them.

"What happened? Where are all the animals?" Bobbi asked.

"Weekend off. Everyone's in fine form," Mom said. "No reason for us to keep them. Their owners will do a better job."

Bobbi pouted. "I really liked them."

"Come back another time," Mom said. "This is rare."

I stepped off the stairs. "Why are you here?"

"You weren't at the arena today. So I came over."

"You didn't need to. I needed a break."

"Then let's take a break. We'll go shopping. We'll get your hair cut and buy new clothes."

Mom grabbed her purse. "Here. Take my credit card. Don't go too nuts. I've been trying to get Cooper to go shopping with me."

"So I can pick out stuff for you," I said. Mom watched too much *Queer Eye*. She thought that having a gay son meant I could help her pick fashions to make her look good. I couldn't. Anything I told her to wear she said clashed or looked cheap.

"You need new clothes," Mom said. "Get some lunch too. On me." She nearly shoved us out the door. I didn't have time to say no. I was stuck with Bobbi for the afternoon.

As soon as we were in her car, Bobbi said, "Dax texted yesterday. You went back to the arena."

"I left something behind."

"He said you were upset."

"I'm not."

Bobbi slowed down when the light ahead

of us turned yellow. A car sped around us and honked.

"What is it? Guy problems?" she asked.

I looked out the window. "I'm fine."

"Was it me telling you about Pesh? Did I share too much?" The light turned green. She pulled forward. "I know I do that sometimes."

I shook my head. "It isn't any of my business."

"Is it the guy commenting on all your posts? I saw old pics of you two. He was your boyfriend, wasn't he? It's obvious from the photos and his comments."

I sighed. "We broke up when his family moved."

"That sucks," Bobbi said. She was quiet a while. "I'm thinking of breaking up with Pesh. Don't say anything. Not to him. Or anyone."

"Wait. What?"

Bobbi pulled into the mall parking lot. "I thought about it after you and I talked. Pesh and I did it. But we still aren't together. We're not texting more. We're not hanging out more. He hasn't even tried to do it again. It all feels the same. I don't know if I want to keep seeing someone I'm not crazy for. Or who isn't crazy for me. I like Pesh. He's cool. But I don't know if it's enough."

After Pesh and I hooked up, we'd been all over each other. We couldn't keep our hands off each other. We'd find excuses to be alone. Up until yesterday, that's how we were. But maybe that was it between Pesh and me. Maybe it was all only physical.

"I want to feel excited around him. I want to tear his clothes off. I want him to feel the same. I don't think we do." Bobbi pulled into a parking spot. "Guys are hard to figure out."

I laughed. "Not really. We're hungry. We're tired. We're turned on. That's it."

"That can't be it."

"Really?"

Bobbi laughed too. "Okay. Let's shop. Let's see if we can get some new clothes and turn some guys on."

Chapter 20

Light the Lamp

We both got our hair cut. Bobbi told me she always got a barber to cut her hair. We both tried on a hundred different things. We each bought a couple of new outfits. Bobbi had a thing for cat clothes. She told the salesperson she liked cats but not animal print. I wore a new pair of jeans and a blue knit sweater out of the store. Bobbi said they made the most of my height and toned down my redness. I even bought new sneakers.

On the way home, Bobbi turned into the arena's lot.

"What are we doing here?" I asked.

"Practice is over. I said I'd pick up Pesh. I'll still drive you home. Besides, it's a total waste to look this good and not show off." Bobbi opened her car door.

"I can grab the streetcar home," I said.

"You've got all those bags. Hurry up. There's someone in there who needs to see you." Bobbi got out of the car.

I followed and caught up in a few strides. I didn't know why she wanted Pesh to see my new look so badly.

"Dax!" Bobbi waved at him as soon as we were in the arena.

Dax was wiping down the benches. He smiled at us. One dimple showed when he did. I hadn't noticed before. It made him look tilted. It was cute.

Dax said, "You look . . . cleaned up."

"Thanks. You're a real charmer." Bobbi

giggled. "You should feel Cooper's sweater. It's so soft." She nearly shoved Dax at me.

Dax stroked the sleeve. "It is." He quickly let go.

"I'll see what's keeping Pesh." Bobbi started toward the locker rooms.

"You can't. The team is still in there," he said.

"I'll go," I said. I couldn't avoid seeing Pesh forever. At least I didn't have to do it in front of Bobbi and Dax.

Bobbi bit her lip. She looked like she wanted to say something. Dax went back to wiping down seats.

When I was halfway down the hall, the door to the change room opened. A bunch of chatter hit me. It was followed by the smell of sweat and steamy showers. The team filed past me. They greeted me and said goodbye all in the same breath.

I stepped inside. Pesh was pulling a shirt on. He spotted me as his head came through the neck hole. His eyes got wide. A hint of his smirk appeared.

"You still mad?" he asked.

I shook my head.

"Good." Pesh stepped over his hockey bag. "It all happened so fast with Bobbi. I wasn't planning on it. I still should have told you. Things are okay again. Right?"

"I don't know," I said.

He pushed the door closed. He stepped close to me. My back was against the door. My front was against him. He put a hand on either side of me.

"You look great." He reached up and smoothed my hair. He smelled like soap and body spray.

I stared into his eyes. He kissed my neck. I tilted my head.

"We shouldn't," I whispered.

"No one's around."

"Bobbi's upstairs."

"And?" He reached for my belt. It was new.

Bobbi had picked it.

I grabbed his hand and stopped him. "We need to talk about what's going on between us."

Pesh gave a full smirk. "You mean this?" He rubbed against me.

I put both hands on his shoulders and pushed him back. "Is it just fooling around?"

"I told you I like you."

"I'm gay. I don't want to hide."

"There are no gay guys in hockey," Pesh shot. "You know how this sport is. I can't be with Bobbi and you. I can't be with you at all. I'd ruin my shot at a career."

"Bobbi said that hockey needs guys to come out. She says there are fans and kids who need to see someone like me. Someone like you," I argued.

"Bobbi isn't thinking right. She thinks because agents are coming out, it's time for that. It isn't. Hockey isn't ready. She's wrong."

"What if she's not? I can be gay and get drafted."

"What about me?" Pesh asked. "Tell me, how many Sri Lankan guys do you see playing hockey? How many not-white guys? And how are they treated when they do go pro? If their teams lose, they're blamed. If they win, they're attacked. I'm already fighting for my shot harder than any of the other guys because of that. I can't add liking guys and liking girls. I can't fight both, but I don't have a choice over the other like you do. I might as well never pick up a stick again. I'd be done."

I didn't know what to say. Part of me knew Pesh was right. I only had to be one thing. I only had one fight. And I'd chosen to be quiet about who I was when I'd joined a new team. Because it kept me safer. "I'm sorry," I said. "I didn't see it that way."

Pesh looked away and shrugged. "Weren't you having fun sneaking around?"

"I was," I admitted. I wasn't now.

"We had fun with this too." He rubbed the front of my pants with his other hand. "Things don't need to change. They're working. We just need to play this smart."

I moved his hands away. "They can't keep working. Not this way."

"Fine," Pesh spat. "You can ruin your shot at going pro. I'm not ruining mine. The odds are already stacked against me. I'm not about to let you or anyone else stop me."

"I'm not trying to stop you." I went to grab his wrist. "I'm on your team."

"Don't!" He pulled it away. "I want this too much."

He left the locker room. I didn't try to stop him.

It was clear. He didn't want me that much.

Chapter 21

Slashing

Pesh and I didn't talk at practices over the next week. They were rough. The next two games, held in our own arena, were rough too. The arena was packed. The last games of the season. The finals. Our friends and families filled the place. We lost both games. With three wins each, the game in Grand Bend would be the last. Whoever won would take it all.

I tried to get Pesh alone. I figured we could smooth things over. I figured if maybe we talked, we could find a way around things. We could fight together to make room in hockey to be who we were. But he was always with the other guys. And I didn't actually have a plan. I knew a lot of what Pesh had said about hockey was right and I didn't know how to change it or help him.

As far as I knew, Bobbi and Pesh were still together. Bobbi kept offering to drive me home from practices. I always found an excuse. My social media was growing stronger, thanks to her. She posted a lot of photos of me. She was right — my ex made comments on all of them.

I texted Pesh that I wanted to talk. He didn't reply.

I gave up trying to talk to Pesh. I went to Coach two days before the final game. I asked him if I could bunk alone for the last away game. I told him I needed my own room to get ready. Really, I couldn't think about being in a room alone with Pesh and him not talking to me. Coach agreed to let me bunk alone.

The afternoon before our last game, I sat at the front of the bus and finished my homework. Bobbi had been a huge help. No surprise, she was good at numbers.

She and I had made a plan for me to come out on my feeds. It was going to be through little stuff we'd add into posts. She'd already built me up as a goalie like any other guy. A tough hockey player who could take a puck. The boss of the crease. She wanted me relatable. She wanted it to still be me. She said all I had to do was give her the go-ahead. Letting people know I was gay was letting them see more of me. It was one more fact about me and that was it.

Part of me was holding off because I was scared to do it so publicly. Part of me was holding off because I knew that once I came out online, Pesh would want nothing to do with me. And I still wanted things to be better between us.

When we arrived in Grand Bend, we used the high school's arena for an evening practice. Then it was lights out. Coach Chug had been clear about a strict curfew. He wanted us all in bed and rested. There wasn't going to be any funny business. Our parents and friends would drive up in the morning for the last game.

I showered. In only a towel, I flopped on the bed. I flicked on the TV and watched some reality show about people who bought all their groceries with coupons. It was not good. It was also great.

There was a banging on my door.

"Hold on." I looked for my pants as I pulled the towel tighter around me.

Pesh's face looked weird through the peephole. I opened the door a little. The chain was on.

"I need to come in," Pesh said. "It's past lights out. If Coach catches me, we're both going to get it."

"Then go back to your room."

"I want to talk."

"I've been trying to talk to you," I said.

"I'm ready now. And I can't talk through a door."

I sighed as I closed the door. I undid the chain and let Pesh inside.

He threw the deadbolt and chain on when he came in. I sat on the bed. He eyed me up and down, his eyes resting on the towel. I put my hands over my lap to cover myself more.

"There will be scouts tomorrow," Pesh said.

"Probably."

"I need to play well. I need to look good."

"Then play well. Why are you here, Pesh?"

He stood in front of me. "Once more. For luck."

"Seriously?"

"Please. I want to win. I need you to do that. I never stopped liking you, Coop." Pesh leaned down. "Let me stay the night. I need you." His eyes were big in the light from the TV. I had missed him.

He kissed me gently. I kissed back. I ran my hand down Pesh's back into his pants. I slid my hand into the back of his underwear.

Then I remembered the red panties. I yanked my hand out of his pants.

"You came to talk," I said. "We should talk. We could work together. Support one another. Maybe we could change things. Not just for us. For everyone."

"Do you really believe that?" Pesh spat. "Are you that dumb?"

"I'm not dumb," I said.

"Then be smart. Accept we have a good thing going. We both get what we need out of this. We're getting regular action. We're winning games. You can't have more. Not in this game."

"I don't want to play that game. I never signed up for it."

"So much drama!" Pesh backed up. "I'm tired of this. We were having a good time. You're acting like such a little —"

I got up. My towel dropped. I made myself as tall as I could. "Like what? Choose your words carefully," I warned him.

Pesh huffed as he stomped to the door. "Whatever. You'll be sorry," he said as it slammed behind him.

Chapter 22

Slap Shot

My phone buzzed me awake the next morning. The vibrating was constant.

I switched on the screen and squinted. I rubbed my fist against my eyes. My alerts were full.

I tapped open my social media apps. There was a picture of me on the ice. Someone had put a filter over it. The photo was coloured like a rainbow. *Plays Gay* was written across it.

I didn't stop to think. I pulled up my

contacts and hit dial.

"Bobbi here," the voice on the other end of the line said.

"What did you do? You said you'd wait until I said it was okay! This is not okay!" I nearly yelled into the phone.

"Cooper? What are you talking about?"

"My feed is going nuts. Why would you do this?"

"Let me pull over." I heard the ticker on her car going. "I'm on my way to watch your last game. Let me look. Oh, crap!"

Neither of us spoke.

"Cooper, I didn't do this," Bobbi finally said.

"You were the only one with my passwords."

"I swear. I would never. Not to you. Or anyone. I can take this down."

"The damage is already done."

"You have to believe me." Bobbi sounded like she might cry.

For some reason, I did believe her. Bobbi

wasn't like that. I knew that. Bobbi was smart and planned things. We had become friends. Bobbi wouldn't do this to a friend. "If it wasn't you —" I said.

"It wasn't!"

"I know that now," I said. "But who?"

I remembered. Last night.

I said, "I have to go."

"Wait. You believe me?"

"Yes. I'm sorry. I shouldn't have blamed you. I'll see you at the game." I hit the end call button.

I threw on some clothes. Without brushing my teeth or fixing my hair, I went downstairs. I marched into the breakfast buffet. I grabbed Pesh by the shoulder where he was standing in line getting eggs.

"Outside," I said.

He smirked. "Bring my food to the table, Brian." Pesh shoved his plate into Brian's hands.

We walked out of the hotel side by side. My fists were balled up. We were silent the whole way. When we were far enough away from the doors, I said, "Why?"

Pesh smirked. "Why what?"

Normally I'd go red. Or my mouth would go dry. Or I'd get a headache or feel sick. Instead, I gritted my teeth and grabbed him by the front of his shirt.

"Let me go," Pesh said. "I warned you. I told you you'd be sorry."

"This is low, Pesh. How did you even hack my accounts?"

"Bobbi had your passwords written down. I saw them and snapped a photo. Isn't this what you wanted?"

"To be outed online? Why would I want that?"

"You wanted to be an out and proud hockey player. You said kids needed to see someone like you. You thought hockey was ready. I helped. I gave you a push."

I gripped the front of Pesh's shirt harder. "That's not true. Why?"

Pesh tried to shove me away. I held tight.

He glared. "If you think being the gay goalie will help you get drafted like Bobbi says, then fine. It will help you. But I think no one will draft a gay guy onto their team. You're my only real competition for a spot. I want the scout to draft me. I told you nothing would stop me. I'm taking every shot I can. I had to take you out. So if it's between the Brown guy and the gay guy, which is worse?"

I shoved Pesh away.

"Let's hope the guys don't get weirded out in the locker room," Pesh said. "See you on the ice."

I walked away and pulled out my phone. My eyes blurred with tears. I wiped my fist across my eyes as I headed in a side door to the hotel and went up to my room.

Inside, I pulled up my texts with Pesh. I took a screenshot. I sent it to him. I followed it with the photos of the two of us in bed together. I texted: *Two can play.* I powered off my phone.

What Pesh had said about the other guys stuck in my head. I didn't want the guys to feel strange changing around me. I didn't want someone to say or do something. I got as much of my gear on as I could walk to the arena in before I left my room. I was sweaty by the time I arrived, but I was ready to take the ice in almost no time. No one had to feel weird about changing around me.

Coach Chug's pre-game pep talk went right by me. I wasn't listening. I glanced at Pesh. His jaw was clenched. He looked only at Coach.

I stared into the crowd. There were some faces I knew. Bobbi was with my parents. They waved. One more person waved too. Dax. I waved back.

No one scored the first period. A lot of shots were taken on our net. I saved them. Where was my defence? It felt like they'd left me on my own. There shouldn't have been so many shots.

Second period was the same. Except both teams scored. We got ahead by one point in the beginning of the third. By the end of it, it was a tie. Overtime.

We took a small break. I downed some water. Some of the guys were chatting. None were talking to me. We hit the ice.

As I got into position, Brian skated over to the net.

"You've got to be tired," he said. "You've been blocking a lot of shots."

"I was worried it was just me thinking that," I replied.

"Nope. Defence sucks today. I know I'm supposed to be scoring on the other team. But I'm going to protect you and our net as much as I can. I've got you." Brian held out his stick between his padded gloves.

I held my own stick up. We bumped fists. I reached out and pulled Brian into a hug. He hugged me back and hit me on the shoulder before he skated away.

Overtime ticked down. I did my best to keep the puck out of my zone. I barely managed it. Brian was doing his best too. He skated between the other players and stole the puck. But we were all tired.

The other team was still far enough away that I was out of my crease when I saw the shot. It went high. There was nothing in its way. I could see it sailing through the air. It went to my left. I knew if I didn't stop it, it wouldn't go over the crossbar or hit it. It would go straight into the net. It would be the winning goal.

I pushed hard. I flipped my stick up. I dove. The crowd was silent.

The puck hit my stick while I was in the air. I landed on my side on the ice an instant later.

Cheers filled the arena.

Brian recovered the puck. The other team must have been sure it was going in. They didn't move fast enough. When they did, Brian was ready. He passed to Pesh, who was open. Pesh skated like mad. On the breakaway, he spun, faked, scored.

There was still time left in the period. The clock ticked down. But neither team got close to another goal again.

My team was on me when the buzzer went. They jumped all over me.

"That save was epic!" Brian screamed.

Pesh was by the boards. Dale and Chris and more guys jumped on me. When I looked for Pesh again, he was gone.

Pesh wasn't in the locker room when all of us got there. The energy was high. We all calmed down enough to shower and change.

When I came up into the arena, Mom was the first to rush over and hug me.

Dad wasn't far behind. "You'll make me a hockey fan after all," he said as he hugged me.

Bobbi waited before she squeezed me too. "I got that save on video. Well, Dax did. I posted it. Did you look at the other post?"

I groaned.

"But did really you look at it? The comments are pretty supportive. People are on your side. Most of them, anyway. I know it wasn't what we planned. But it's okay. I can work with it."

"We can work with it," I said.

Dax stood at a distance. I waved him over.

"I think you need something better than a hot chocolate after that win," he said.

I felt really good. We had just won! I moved in and hugged him. I thought it would be strange with our height difference, but Dax was a solid guy. I lifted him off his feet.

"You're not backing out of that hot chocolate now," I said as I put him down again.

Bobbi turned her phone around so we could see the screen. It was a pic of me hugging Dax. He looked shocked, mid-air. I had a silly grin across my face.

"You two look great together," she said. "I'm going to post this with the victory photos."

Chapter 23

Final Overtime

I had to get my stuff from my hotel room before we took the bus back home to Toronto. I could have gone with my parents. Or with Bobbi and Dax. But, because of Brian, I finally felt like part of the team. It felt right taking the bus back with the other guys.

Pesh leaned against the wall by my room.

I walked past, opened my door and went inside. I began to close the door. I didn't want to talk to him. There was nothing to say.

No way he could explain it. And I didn't want to be angry. I didn't want to cry. I didn't want anything. He'd screwed me over by putting up that post. All that had been between us was screwing. We were done.

He stuck his foot in the way of the door.

"If you have something else to say, say it from out there," I told him.

"I spoke to Chug. We got offers. Both of us. Can I come in?"

"You don't need to."

"Fine. About the post. I know I can't undo it. I know I can't make it right." Pesh stared up at me through his lashes.

I held the door firmly. He blocked it with his body. He put his hand on top of mine.

"I was mad," he said.

"So what?"

"Open the door, Coop," Pesh whispered. "Things were going good. We can make them work again. We'll figure it out. Together this time." He slid his hand up my arm and squeezed my bicep.

It felt nice to have him touch me again. Familiar. But I hadn't forgotten what he did. I couldn't. I pushed his hand off. "No. Not after everything."

"But those pictures," Pesh said.

So he was here because of the photos of us together. That was the only reason. Not because he cared about me or missed me. Not because he was sorry. Not because he shouldn't have done it. He was scared.

"They're private." I relaxed my grip on the door. "They'll stay that way."

Pesh's shoulders relaxed. He stepped out of the way a little. I felt sad I hadn't been wrong. Pesh really had only been here to keep those pics from going online.

"But you have to agree to this," I said. "Either you tell Bobbi everything or you break up with her."

Pesh laughed. "I don't think so."

I pushed the door and forced him out.

"Then I'll show her the photos and our texts. I'll tell her everything. I'll let her help me choose whether we put them up online."

"She'll hate you," he said.

"Maybe," I replied. "But that's the play I'm going with. Unless you agree."

"Whatever. I'm done with this team. I'm done with you. I'm done with her too. Just delete those photos and texts." Pesh pulled his foot out of the door's way. He walked down the hallway and around the corner.

When I got on the bus, he wasn't on it.

Chapter 24

Gong Show

The bus ride back to Toronto took longer than expected. As soon as we hit the 401, the highway was a parking lot.

Jon, a younger player who had ridden the bench all season, told the story of our win again. Everyone had taken a turn telling it but me.

"What was going on in your head when you dove for that shot?" Jon asked when he was done.

I shook my head. "I had to block the puck. That's it."

"Pure focus." Jon nodded.

Brian slid into the seat beside me. "About your post from this morning," he said. "Why do it right before the final game?"

The rest of the guys turned in their seats to face me. The bus inched forward. The Toronto city limits sign came into view.

My mouth went dry. No one had said anything about the post. And I couldn't tell them what Pesh had done. Not when I couldn't tell them why he had done it. "Bobbi's been helping me with social media. We planned something. It wasn't anyone's fault. It went all wrong. It wasn't meant to go up." It wasn't exactly true. It wasn't exactly a lie. "I wasn't trying to keep a secret. Or have some big reveal."

Brian traded looks with the other guys. He said, "We suck. We should have been a better team to you. We should have made sure you or any other guy knew we'd be cool."

I nodded. Brian held out his hand. We fist-bumped. Then each of the guys took turns coming over and fist-bumping me.

We got off the bus and grabbed our gear from the storage below. I stretched my arms and legs.

"Did your parents come to pick you up?" Brian asked.

I shook my head. "I'll take the streetcar. First I need a bathroom. I'll catch you later."

Brian trotted over to his mom, who was waiting to give him a hug. I went into the arena and ducked into the nearest washroom. As I was leaving, I heard voices. It was Pesh and Bobbi. I ducked back into the washroom.

"Your parents must be so happy," Bobbi said.

"You'd think," Pesh replied. "They weren't even there. They think this is only a game. But now I'll go to a better school. I'll be on a better team. Everything will be better and new."

"Everything?" Bobbi asked. "Maybe you need a new girl too."

"What?" Pesh said. "Where did that come from?"

"You know where," Bobbi sighed. "You didn't pick up my calls for a week. You didn't answer my texts. This is the first time I've seen you. We've barely been talking since we had sex."

"I needed to keep my head in the game."

"I know," Bobbi said. "And I understand. I'm not mad. I know how much you want to go pro. You'll do it. But you need to stay in the game. Not to worry about a girl who isn't even your girlfriend."

Pesh laughed. It was too loud. Too fake. "I get drafted, and you dump me?"

"I can't dump you. We were never together. Not really. I want you to be happy. I want you to get what you want. That isn't me. I really do hope everything is newer and better for you."

Pesh didn't answer. I ducked behind the bathroom door more as Bobbi walked past.

I waited because I couldn't sneak out. I heard Pesh kick the bottom of the vending machine. Then the bathroom door pushed in. I dropped my bag and stepped back.

Pesh and I stood facing each other.

His lashes were clumped together. His eyes looked shiny.

"I didn't dump her. But we're not together," he said. "Is that enough for you? Isn't that what you wanted?"

"This isn't what I wanted," I said. I meant it. I didn't want to see Pesh hurt. I did earlier. Not now. He wanted to be a pro hockey player so bad. Everything he did was to get there. And he felt everything was against him. The odds. His parents. Liking a guy. How he looked. And he couldn't control any of it. Not even if he practised harder than any other guy. He asked me what people would think was worse in hockey, me being gay or him being Sri Lankan. I couldn't know what every person out there thought. I knew what I saw in front of me.

Even though Pesh had got what he wanted, things were worse for him than for me.

I reached into my pocket and pulled out my phone. I pushed at the screen before I turned the phone around to him. I hit the trash icon. Delete.

"Why did you do that? You can't get back at me now," he said.

I shook my head. Pesh didn't need to be hurt. Not even if he hurt me. Nothing would get fixed that way. We'd just take shots at each other. And he was hurting enough already.

"I would have kept them," he said.

"I know." I picked up my hockey gear. "But I don't need them. I want things to be better for you too. Getting rid of those pics was the only way I could see to make it better for you." I pressed my back against the wall and slid past Pesh.

Pesh turned to me. He wiped the back of his arm across his eyes. "I'm —"

"I know," I said.

Chapter 25

Post Game

Bobbi helped me with my math homework over the next few weeks. I needed it. But I was getting better with her help. She'd come over to my house. Any animal we had staying with us seemed ready to curl up with her. If she didn't go into PR, she could become a vet. She had the clothes for it.

I didn't tell her about Pesh and me. Maybe I should have. Maybe she had a right to know. I could only see it hurting her. I didn't want to hurt anyone.

Bobbi called me on a Saturday afternoon and told me we needed to meet up. She had business to talk about. She suggested the coffee shop by the arena.

"We need to look at your offers," she said. "You need to make a choice if you're going to the next level. I made a list."

I had received more than one offer and I had decided to take one. I didn't know which yet. I wanted to accept the right one. I loved hockey. I was good at it. If I could go pro, I was going to. And I wasn't going to hide who I was.

"We need to pick the best fit for you," said Bobbi. "Being out this early in your career is a bonus. If you went pro first, you might not be able to come out. At least not easily. You'll go in gay. Whoever posted on your account did you a favour. They probably didn't mean to. But they might have. Hockey will have to adjust to you. Not the other way around." Bobbi finished her pink drink with extra whip.

"This place does refills. Don't they?"

"I'll buy you a fresh one if they don't. Do you have any strong feelings about any of the teams? Who would you pick?"

The shop's door opened. Fresh, cool early spring air came in. Dax came with it.

"Only a sudden strong feeling for hot chocolate," Bobbi said. "Dax. What a surprise."

"Not really. You know I got a part-time job here," he said.

Until I heard him speak again, I didn't realize how much I missed Dax's voice.

"I didn't know you were working today. It's not like I know when your shifts are." Bobbi rolled her eyes but smiled. She turned her phone on and looked at it. "I've got to go. I'll be late."

"For a hot date or something?" I joked.

"Or a new client?" Dax asked.

Bobbi blushed. "Both. Don't look at me like that. I know I should have learned my lesson with Pesh. Don't mix business and dating. Brian asked for some advice. Then he asked me out."

"I like Brian," Dax said.

I agreed. "He's a good guy."

Bobbi stayed red. "And a good kisser. We're trying to take it slow. It's been hard."

"No strings? Casual?" I asked.

Bobbi grinned. "All sorts of strings. He's already calling himself my boyfriend." She packed her new bag in the shape of a Hello Kitty head and left.

"Do you have time to sit?" I asked Dax.

"I've got an hour before I start. I like to be early." He took the seat across from me.

"Can I get you a drink?" I asked.

"I thought I owed you the hot chocolate."

"But you're not working in the snack shack anymore."

"No," Dax said. "And I won't be again. I got my dream gig in the arena next season. I'll be on the speakers calling out the games. The guy who did it is off to college."

"You have the perfect voice for it." I could feel my cheeks and the tips of my ears getting warm.

"You like it?" Dax gave me his tilted smile. *"The puck is in the air! It's driving right to the net! Cooper dives! He blocks it! The puck is passed down the ice. They score! There's no coming back! Cooper wins the game!"*

I knew I was red. Flaming red. Burning hot. I looked at Dax's dimpled smile and broad shoulders. I could still hear him in my mind.

I swallowed. Then I took a deep breath. "Maybe we could take the streetcar together sometime after one of your shifts," I suggested. "Maybe you don't have to get off at your stop."

"Why not?" Dax asked. His voice was low. I could have dove into it like I dove for that puck.

"You could come to my place. For dinner. Our house isn't fancy. It's usually filled with sick animals and medical stuff. Not for any creepy reason. My parents are vets."

"Are you asking me out?" Dax had stopped smiling.

"Yes. I don't know if you're into that. Or

into guys. Or me. If you're not, sorry. I didn't mean anything."

Dax reached across the table and took my hand. "I'd love to. I'm done at six. Is that too soon? Do you want to stick around?"

"I'd love to too." I felt dumb as soon as I said it.

Dax turned red. "I could sneak behind the counter and make us two hot chocolates. I do owe you."

I turned my hand over and laced my fingers between Dax's.

He stared down.

"Is this okay?" I asked. "In public like this?"

He gulped and nodded. "Very okay."

"Maybe you can make those hot chocolates in a few minutes," I said. "I'm not in a rush. Tell me about your new jobs. I'm sticking around for a while."

Acknowledgements

It is with gratitude that I acknowledge the following:

Karen Spafford-Fitz for her generosity and friendship in helping this story find its home.

Kat Mototsune, my editor and friend who is tributed with the artistic direction of Bobbi's clothing, as well as the team at Lorimer for all their help and hard work.

The Canadian Childrens' Writing community for embracing and supporting me as a new author, but especially those who have become friends I rely on and value.

My family and my friends who always bolster and inspire me.

My thanks and love to you all.

Author's Note

At the time of writing, there were no openly gay men playing professional hockey. As the book was going to print, an NHL agent, Bayne Pettinger, came out. I am proud to see change happening, proud of Bayne and proud and thankful to the editors at Lorimer for allowing me to adjust the text with only minutes left in the game.